HEART OF SIN

AN ELEMENTAL MONARCHS COMPANION
NOVEL

LINN TESLI

INSPIRERT PUBLISHING

To the wonderful people in my life—for your courage and strength, but above all for your flaws, compassion, endurance, wit and vulnerabilities: All that which makes you, not only strong, but human.

CHAPTER ONE

A SHEET OF DUST SETTLED IN THE ARENA WHILE SIN WAITED for her opponent. The chip in the sandstone wall to her left reminded her of her first kill. Was it really twelve years ago already? She could no longer recall his name, though she could still remember the sound of his head crushing. He had been older than her, perhaps seven or eight, and he'd had the ability to transform the density of metal. It hadn't done him much good, however. He might have ruined her first sword but her fists had been tougher than his.

The dirt crunched between her toes as she adjusted her stance. She knew every crack and scratch in the circular wall of stone. Every speck of dust surrounding her was an old acquaintance, and the familiar smell of iron and copper made her eager for the deathmatch. She couldn't know her own skin any more than she knew these grounds. And her opponents suffered for it.

The entire House of Spirit—her house—was seated

at one side, the House of Air—her opponent's house—on the other. In the center sat all five Grand Masters—watching—as they always were during a deathmatch. Training matches had smaller audiences.

The five Silverling masters wore the same outfits every day, matching robes separated only by the colors of their houses. Their silver-tinted skin shone in the light of the waning sun. She knew them well but Master Matteo had always stood out among the others. He was larger, with broad shoulders, cloaked in silver and purple. She nodded his way and got a tilt of his chin in response. She frowned, and a few strands of lavender-colored hair fell over her eyes. The masters had yet to grant her what she wanted most—a mission of her own. Soon though, they had to. But first, she had to take one more life, and then—come morning—she would be granted her position as an official daughter of the order, through the Rite of the Dragon.

Only moments remained before the sound of the gong would announce the battle to begin.

A shadow stretched through the arched entrance, followed by a boy dressed in black and teal colors. Sin almost shook her head. He was probably her age, though small, nothing but skin and bones by the looks of him. His fragile frame wasn't what she had become accustomed to in the arena. Most of her opponents had been well trained, and their bodies bore witness of their training. The boy in front of her didn't look like he had trained a day in his life, which was strange by all accounts, as new fledglings were never older than nine.

The boy walked up to his appointed mark, a line of blood in the dirt from the last defeated fledgling, then stopped and took the traditional bow toward the Grand Masters. At the very least, he was familiar with customary behavior. The slight breeze tugged at his wild, tangerine-colored hair; it was longer than hers, reaching all the way to his shoulders.

The sound of the gong sent tremors through the ground.

Sin adjusted her stance while staring straight at her opponent. His azurite-blue eyes were determined, but they would soon lack any emotions at all. The sense of both awe and fear was almost tangible as her opponent attempted to mirror her motions. He made the first move. It was foolish and predictable, leaving him completely exposed for an attack. She merely side-stepped as the tip of his sword came at her abdomen. She twirled on her feet as the boy stumbled to the ground behind her.

The noise of the spectators gasping and shouting entered Sin's mind. She blocked out the sounds as best she could.

It would have been over in another heartbeat. Sin could have had his head right then, but to what end, other than adding another mark to her shoulders? The onlookers were possible teammates and future opponents. Moreover, the masters were not interested in a clean kill. They wanted to see what the pair of them were capable of, and Sin was going to show them. Instead of swinging her blade for a lethal blow, she gripped the boy by his hair and forced him back down as he tried to get up, sending him flat on the ground. It gave her time, so she opened her mind. The surging energy of magic shot through her, making her heart pump like she had been training all day instead of minutes. She reached for the boy's power and staggered backward at the impact of what felt like hitting a wall. The sword clanked at the ground as her hands flew to her temples. Her head was pounding. She saw none of the usual colors surrounding Magicals. In fact, she sensed no magic at all. What was he—an Unspelled? Why was he here then?

The boy stood, dusting himself off. He picked up Sin's sword and offered it back to her. She paused, then grabbed the hilt and raised the blade over her head. Her powers were useless and there would be no show for the masters watching. It was time to end it. She took a step backward and hesitated. Why would she kill an Unspelled, and why would the masters want her to do so? It made no sense. Still, he had been placed in the arena with her, so there had to be a reason. Perhaps they were testing her resolve, trying to find out how far she would go? Or maybe they wanted to know that they could trust her to make the right decisions? Perhaps this was her final test, to see if she was so corrupted by her magic that she couldn't tell friend from foe?

A Protector wasn't supposed to kill the Unspelled, but rather protect them. She was about to swing her sword for a non-lethal blow when the sound of the gong made her stop. The fight had ended with no kills

—that was a first. The boy backed up and gave a slight bow to the masters, then to Sin. Why had they made them stop? Sin glanced at the Grand Masters as Matteo stood. He moved away from the others and descended the stairwell like a ghost gliding on the water before he entered the arena.

"Well done, Ward." He patted the boy on his shoulder then turned to Sin. "Come now, both of you. There are matters to discuss."

"Yes, Master," Sin and the boy said simultaneously.

Sin sheathed her sword in annoyance. This was not how she had envisioned her last deathmatch before the Rite. She scowled at the boy. His hair was tousled and he was smiling at Matteo. He should be dead, yet the masters had spared him—she had spared him. Why was he so special? He didn't have magic; perhaps that was why.

The boy caught her gaze and motioned closer, extending his hand. "My name is Ward. Nice to meet you, though I suppose the circumstances could have been nicer." His eyes shifted over the spectators dispersing to find their way out of the arena on the other side.

She grimaced but took his hand. "Sinyara."

Matteo waved at them from the arched entry point of the arena, and they fell in step. They followed him in silence across the upper bailey and into the east tower, continuing onto the battlements of the castle on Mount Fyra. The lights from the city of Valano twinkled dimly in the distance, past the sand dunes of the Caradrean plains, which stretched out from the foot of the mountain to the east. Further south, Sin could just about make out the shape of the city of Cazib. She knew everything there was to know about this land—the Land of Air—yet she had rarely stepped foot off the mountain since her arrival, apart from during such training sessions as hunting, tracking and riding. Her memory of what came before was a fog. All she remembered was Matteo's silver-tinted face in a doorway, his purple lips smiling at her.

The squawk of a falcon caught her attention. The bird swooped down to perch on Sin's shoulder.

"Hey there, Nefero," she said with her softest voice. She stroked the falcon on its back and sighed. "I have missed you."

Nefero leaned his head over her ear, hiding underneath her short tresses as Sin gripped the edge of the crenel with both hands, awaiting Matteo's instructions.

"You have been paired as a team," Matteo said.

"Him?" Sin blurted.

Ward stared at his feet. "I'm honored," he mumbled.

"As you should be. And so should you, Sinyara." Matteo gave her a stern look. "Ward here is special. He will be a great asset on your first mission." He gave Ward a pat on the back.

She brightened at the mention of a mission. She had longed for this day for years. Still, why did Ward get to come?

"You saw him out there. He can't fight, and I sensed no powers."

Matteo chuckled, placing a hand on her free shoulder. Nefero was still occupying the other one. "That's because Ward is a Shield. He absorbs the powers of other Magicals, rendering them useless to the owner. It really is quite clever, not to mention useful for what you are about to face. And now we know that not even you, a Seeker, could tell him apart. Learn to know each other. I will gather the rest of your team and give you more information after the Rite tomorrow." Matteo walked away, leaving Sin and Ward on the battlements.

So he was a Magical after all. A Shield. Sin couldn't remember having met anyone with an ability like that in her twelve years on Mount Fyra. And there were hundreds of children there.

The boy angled away from her to lean over the crenels. "It's exciting, isn't it? I can't wait to get to the ground and see where our mission will take us."

A Shield? Sin couldn't quite wrap her head around it. The boy looked so fragile. Though if Matteo said he was an asset, he probably was.

"How many marks?" she asked as Nefero took flight, soaring out above the plains.

Ward put his chin in his hands, his back slumped. "None."

"None? How can you complete the Rite if you have never killed anyone? Not one?" Every fledgling in Sin's House of Spirit had to get at least ten marks before they were allowed to complete the final rite. This boy had not been part of a single deathmatch, and yet he was about to be handed his first mission, which would also be hers.

"I'm a Shield from the House of Air. I don't have to, I guess." He glanced at her. "How many?"

"You should have been my thirtieth."

SIN LEFT WARD OUTSIDE THE HOUSE OF AIR AND RAN down the steps to the lower bailey. She passed the forge and opened the doors to the stable, inhaling the sweet scent of hay. She greeted each unicorn in passing until she reached the largest stall at the end.

"Hey, Shayfax," Sin cooed. "Anything yet?"

The yellow unicorn shook her head as Sin entered the stall. She stroked one hand over Shayfax's bulging belly. "Mind if I take a look?"

The mare trotted slowly around Sin, allowing her free access. Sin reached out, squeezing gently on the unicorn's nipple, and a spray of thick white milk shot out.

"You're ready! Your foal is lucky that you have all this delicious milk to offer."

The unicorn nickered, content.

"Now we wait." Sin gave her a hug before she went to the far corner of the stall. She arranged the balls of hay to create a makeshift bed, before she lay down, keeping her attention on the mare. The foal would likely arrive sometime during the night. Sin had waited exactly eleven months and four days, and there was no way she was going to miss it. Not even the Rite could keep her away. Her eyelids drooped and she forced them back open. Eventually, however, she could no longer fight it and fell asleep.

SHAYFAX WHINNIED, PROMPTING SIN FROM HER SLEEP.

Her eyes flew open. "Did I miss it?"

She stood, searching for any sign that the foal had arrived without her knowing. The mare turned her back to Sin, a pair of legs sticking out of her. More of the foal was showing, then it stopped moving. Shayfax needed help and Sin rushed over.

"Your foal is stuck. Let me help."

Shayfax whinnied again, much louder this time, and Sin decided to take that as a yes. She pushed one hand along the foal's legs and over his body. Everything felt fine, so it had to be the head preventing the foal from coming loose.

"Hush now," Sin shushed. This was going to be painful and the foal might not survive.

Shayfax neighed and dropped to the ground, forcing Sin to her knees. This was dangerous for the mare as well. But Sin had to at least try.

"I'm so sorry. This will hurt, but you're a strong unicorn. You can do this!" Careful not to hurt either mother or child, Sin grasped the foal as best she could and tried twisting it loose. Her pulse quickened, pounding underneath her skin. She had witnessed many birthings before this one, though this was the first she did by herself. She couldn't fail Shayfax now. The head of the foal suddenly glided over her palm and Sin retracted her arms. The foal gained traction and the head finally appeared. Sin sighed with relief.

The foal's forehead sparkled like gems, a small blanket of diamonds between its ears, though there was no horn in sight. That would come later, if such a thing was allowed on Mount Fyra. Luckily, it wasn't. For all their beauty and companionship, a unicorn with its horn was the most magical being in all of Aradria, and therefore also the most heinous—even more heinous than Sin herself.

The foal sprawled on the ground. It wasn't breathing.

"Shayfax?" Sin prompted. "Your foal needs you."

But Shayfax was too exhausted to turn, so Sin stepped in. She carefully rubbed away the thin sac encasing the foal and discovered it was a boy. She began rubbing his chest with firm motions. It was taking too long. Her hands slid back and forth as she continued rubbing, frantically now. Small beads of sweat coated her skin.

"Come on!" The taste of salt fell on her tongue. Her palms stuck to the foal's fur, and her fingers stiffened at the exercise. "Come on, boy! Breathe!" Panting, she kept rubbing until her arms grew sore. She was just about to give up when the foal gasped for air.

Sin exhaled heavily and wiped her brow with the back of her forearm. That was too close. She sucked air for a few moments then angled her body at the foal. "Good boy!" she said, patting him on his neck.

She carefully pushed him around his mother, so that Shayfax could see him. The mare was exhausted, though the sight of her newborn made her eyes widen, and she leaned in to begin licking him clean. The ground shifted underneath her as Sin staggered to her feet and went over to the trough. She filled a bucket with water and stuck her hands in it, washing her arms. When she was satisfied she was clean enough, she returned to her makeshift bed to stare at the unicorns. If she hadn't been here, the foal would be dead and Shayfax would be mourning. As would Sin. Looking at the unicorns now, however, made her excited about the future. She had saved the foal. Her! For all the wrongs she had done, for all the wickedness in her soul, she had done an act of good. What could be better than saving a child for its mother?

The foal had the same colors as its mother, yellow body and a silver mane. It wouldn't be long before he could stand on his own, and in a couple of months, the first sign of his growing horn would appear. She hoped her mission had ended by then, so she could be back to saw it off every time the tip of his spear grew above his ears. By next winter, it would stop growing altogether. Perhaps then she could start training him. She would ask Matteo if she could have him. Every Protector of the Order was allowed to choose a steed, and she chose him.

"You deserve something special. I think I'll name

you Vilyur." It was a good name, meaning strong of will, which Sin thought was fitting for how the foal had arrived.

Vilyur glanced at her with chestnut eyes. He seemed to like it too. One day she would ride him across the plains on a mission. There would certainly be more to come once she completed her first. No matter what it was, she would get the job done, and Matteo would be proud of her.

Nefero squawked as he came soaring through the stables. He hovered in front of Sin's face, batting his wings and squawking uncontrollably.

Sin waved him off. "Shush. What's wrong with—" Oh no! It was already late in the morning. She scrambled to her feet. "Bloody mother of magic! The Rite!"

The falcon quieted in an instant.

"Thank you." Sin shot to her feet. "Got to run, Shayfax. And congratulations, he's a beauty," she called as she sprinted through the stables. She hurried up the steep stairwell to the upper bailey, rushing across the empty courtyard toward the fledgling houses.

"Where's the Magical?" a boy said. He leaned against the walls of the House of Fire while whetting a large knife.

"The Rite is today. Can't be late."

"We've still got some time. They haven't sounded the gong yet."

The first sound of the gong rang through the air.

"Oops," the boy said, and skipped down the steps. "I guess we're running after all."

They ran side by side, past the House of Air, then the House of Spirit, before the House of the Dragon rose in front of them. Their feet pounded against the cobbled ground in perfect unison. He was fast. Sin had seen him many times before, though they had never spoken. "You're receiving your Rite today, as well?" she asked, gulping down air.

"Not a day too soon. I thought I was going to have to mark my entire body before they would allow me the Rite. Where would I put my fresh dragon-mark then?"

They sprinted up the stairs as the gong sounded a second time, then stopped at the top to catch their breaths. His raven-black hair framed his amber eyes, and he grinned at her.

"Well, then. We made it before the third gong. After you."

Sin raised an eyebrow at him, then carefully pulled the gigantic iron doors open to the point where they could slip inside. The hall was packed. Hundreds of fledglings from all five houses had already found their seats.

"I'm at the front somewhere," Sin said.

"Name's Rip. My house is somewhere in the middle. Catch you later." He sauntered off behind the right row of seats to the wall as Sin made her way down the main aisle to the front.

Matteo gave her a stern look from the podium as she sat down. The other masters all stood by the reverse large mural of the spirit-symbol at the back—four petals aligned to the cardinal points, protected by the circle.

The gong rang for the third time, and the voices stilled. Though it wasn't entirely quiet. Sin could hear the nervous breathing of a girl behind her. Scratching and nail-biting a few rows further back screeched in Sin's ears. A few hundred fledglings were fidgeting in their seats, and the sounds of it made her cringe. When people stopped talking, the world became incessantly loud.

Matteo cleared his voice and took a step forward.

The Rite had begun.

CHAPTER TWO

"Merry meet," Matteo began. "We have gathered here today, on the longest day of the year, to watch a group of fledglings complete their years of training, and accept the Rite of the Dragon." He picked up a torch and went over to an iron vat standing on a tripod in the middle of the podium. The fire roared as soon as the contents met the flame from the torch. As close to the podium as she was, Sin felt the temperature rising only heartbeats later.

Master Zorvaz limped forward with a branding iron the length of both his arms. He'd had that limp for as long as Sin had known him. It was said he had gotten it during an explosion, which nearly claimed his life.

A slight tingle stirred in Sin's chest. She was finally ready to get the mark she had been waiting for. The brand of the dragon.

Zorvaz tapped the head end of the branding iron underneath the vat. "We, the five Grand Masters, acknowledge a fledgling from the House of Fire. Rip, we welcome you."

Sin glanced to the right as Rip bounced from his seat. An Aradrian Protector was about to be born. She wanted it, too. Matteo waved Rip forward and Zorvaz held the iron firmly inside the flames while Rip removed his black tunic, exposing his naked skin. Twenty marks with white scarifications, ten on each shoulder, bore witness to his achievements. His sunburned skin was otherwise covered in cuts and scars. He was a devoted fledgling. Perhaps almost as devoted as her.

Matteo raised his voice. "Rupert, better known as Rip, has been with us since the age of seven. He was considered a menace to the farm he grew up on as his powers often got him in trouble. Now, however, Rip is a young man about to become a Protector. By his sacrifice, Aradria shall fare better than before, and together we shall keep the lands safe from harm." He gestured at Rip. "Bend the knee and accept this gift."

The room seemed to sway as everyone leaned forward in their seats while Rip sat on his knees, facing the assemblage. His shining amber eyes set on Sin's, and his muscles rolled with every expecting pant. She found herself leaning forward, too.

"Do you pledge allegiance to your house, to Mount Fyra, and to your Master Zorvaz for as long as either of you shall exist?" Matteo continued. "And do you pledge to be a faithful servant of the order, to protect

Aradria against any Magicals deemed a threat and to save the Unspelled from harm?"

"I do," Rip said in a low voice.

"Do you fully understand the responsibility placed on your shoulders, the burden you bear, and promise to use the curse of your magic for the good of Aradria, however sinister or sinful it may be?"

"I do!" Rip's voice was louder this time.

"And, finally, do you willingly accept the flame placed on your skin, to wear it with pride, and remember the grace by which you have been allowed to endure despite the magic in your veins?"

"I do!" Rip laughed, his voice ringing through the hall.

"By my position as Head Master of Fyra, Master of the House of Spirit, and an Unspelled Devling, I accept your commitment and grant you the only form of absolution bestowed upon Magicals such as yourself: A place in the Order of Fyra as a Protector."

An audible gasp came from the assemblage as Master Zorvaz lifted the branding iron and approached Rip. Sin held her breath. The iron looked too heavy, especially with that limp. But Zorvaz never faltered.

"By my position as Master of the House of Fire, I brand you with the mark of the dragon," Zorvaz called.

He lifted the iron and pushed it against Rip's shoulder, just below his marks.

Rip screamed, a scream of pain and pleasure all at once. His eyes were full of fire, and even though he was gritting his teeth, he looked like he was smiling the whole time.

Master Zorvaz retracted the iron and placed it back on a metal stand next to the vat.

"Rise," Matteo said. "You are reborn as a Protector of Aradria, a son of the Order of Fyra."

Rip stood to the sound of furious applause.

Sin didn't move—she waited—waited for her turn. It wasn't her name that was called next, however.

Another name was called, then another. The masters repeated the procedure with every fledgling called to the podium. Sin grew increasingly restless. She could feel Matteo's eyes on her, and she knew what he wanted from her. The words she had heard Matteo say so many times over the years echoed in her mind: 'A Protector is a patient servant.' She had to earn her mark, not by force, but by patience.

Another girl walked away from the podium with her new mark when Sin's name was finally announced. She strode as calmly as she could up the steps, then turned to the assemblage. All the countless hours spent studying history, learning to lip-read and track, the years spent wielding a sword and bloodying her knuckles. All of it had led her to this moment.

Sin glanced at the fledglings. All eyes were on her. Some were fairly recent arrivals, the youngest girl not older than four or five. The girl's thick, curly hair was chestnut-colored, matching her large eyes. She smiled at Sin with ruby, heart-shaped lips. Sin wondered briefly at just how deadly this girl would become. Though she might not live for anyone to find out. Every one of the fledglings was dangerous or would become volatile, parasites of Aradria. She loathed them all but, like her, the fledglings served a purpose. Perhaps one day the Protectors would be able to kill off magic altogether, so that the peoples of Aradria may live in peace. That was Sin's dream.

She bowed her head at Master Matteo and took off her shirt so that her torso was covered in nothing but a short woolen top. Matteo nodded back.

"Sinyara, better known as Sin, has been with us since the age of five. Her powers are extraordinary, and so is her mind. It has been my distinct pleasure to watch her grow over the past twelve years. She was a shy child, lost and bewildered, and her powers frightened those around her. They still should, though here on Mount Fyra she has found her way, about to become a Protector. By her sacrifice, Aradria shall fare better than before, and together we shall keep the lands safe from harm." He gestured at Sin. "Bend the knee and accept this gift."

Sin knelt, her heart pounding in her chest. It was happening!

Matteo proceeded to repeat the same words as he had four times already since they convened for the Rite. Though Sin knew every word, they seemed more profound when Matteo was saying them to her.

"I do," she heard herself say.

"By my position as Grand Master of the House of

Spirit, I brand you, Sinyara, with the mark of the dragon."

Sin's muscles tensed. She knew what was coming. The heat in the air touched her first, before the iron pressed against her skin. The pain was excruciating. But Sin knew pain—she lived pain. To allow pain to overcome you was a weakness, and she was not that. Her mouth opened and closed but she didn't scream. Drops of perspiration trickled down her spine, and yet she didn't scream.

The iron was removed and her body swayed.

"Rise," Matteo said. "You are reborn as a Protector of Aradria, a daughter of the Order of Fyra."

Sin forced herself to her feet, her body trembling through the waves of heat and chills journeying through her veins. She was a Protector now. A smile spread on her face. Soon she would embark on her first mission as a true Aradrian Protector, and she could finally do the things she had always been meant for. No Magicals would be allowed to harm Aradria as long as she had a say in the matter.

"That completes the Rite of the Dragon this year," Matteo said. "Merry meet, merry part and merry meet again. And until next time, stay protected."

The applause was deafening as Sin stumbled her way back to her seat. The sound of footsteps grew before they quieted, her own breath replacing the previous noise surrounding her.

When all the other fledglings had cleared out, Matteo came to her side.

"Come, child. I'll take you to the infirmary before you pass out. You look a little pale, and that wound needs cleaning."

Pale? She felt fine. Exhilarated even. The wound did have to be cleaned, however, so she took his arm and he guided her out of the House of the Dragon.

MATTEO WRUNG A CLOTH IN HIS HANDS, THE WATER dripping into the silver bowl underneath. The old infirmary was quiet, the smell of poppy seed and oils infused the room.

"Here," he said. "Show me."

Sin angled her shoulder at him, presenting the fresh branding of the dragon. It stung, but she had waited twelve years to get it. She smiled at Matteo as he began cleaning the soot from her arm. His hands worked in gentle motions, reminding her of her first training sessions.

'Pain teaches us strength,' Matteo always said. The first time she killed, she had cried. A silly, childish thing to do. Matteo had been there, taken her on his lap and told her to be proud. "You were strong, and he was weak," he had said. "Only the strong can protect Aradria." And Sin had decided at that moment that she would be the strongest Protector Aradria had ever seen. If not physically, then at least mentally. Her resolve had doomed opponents physically much stronger than her.

21

Matteo cleared his throat. "Congratulations. You are no longer a fledgling."

"I am what I have always been."

Matteo slanted his head. "The fight was always in you, even as a child. A perfect candidate for an Aradrian Protector."

"Did my parents think so, too?" she asked. They rarely spoke about her past, and Sin was usually all right with that, but she did wonder how her parents would feel knowing she had completed her training. She'd had a life before this, though she had been too young to remember any of it. She couldn't even recall their faces.

Matteo stopped moving for a moment, adding pressure to her shoulder. "Your parents wanted you dead, little bird. I alone saw your true potential. You should not offer them a second thought."

"I apologize." Sin stared at the floor, gritting her teeth. Pain was for the weak. "I owe you my life."

Matteo removed the cloth and hung it over the lip of the bowl. He picked up a smaller bowl of blueish ointment next to it, then carefully smeared the ointment on Sin's skin with the tips of his fingers.

"We look to the future now." He placed the bowl back and knitted his fingers in his lap. "There you are. You will need to do this yourself when you leave. You would usually be cared for here at the grounds, but there is no time to linger. Your mission will begin as soon as your team has been put together."

"My team?"

"Yours and Ward's both, but the team will know that your word is final."

Sin had a sudden urge to give Matteo a hug. She decided against it.

"Thank you, Master. I almost thought you wouldn't even call my name earlier."

He offered her a hand, pulling her to her feet.

"Serves you right for being late. Come, let's walk outside for a while. The moon is bright."

They left the infirmary and headed out to the pathway trailing around the steep mountain, taking them above the fledgling houses and past the battlements, which stretched into the mountainside with nothing but the open air beyond.

A few Vulkan eagles circled the peak, and Nefero flew out from the thick smog to fly down and settle on Sin's shoulder.

Matteo gave Nefero a quick look. "That falcon has clung to you ever since the day I brought you to Mount Fyra. A devotion such as his is precious."

Sin retrieved a handful of bird seeds from the satchel hanging from her belt and presented it to Nefero, who quickly placed his beak in her palm to help himself to his favorite treat.

"People are devious, birds are what they seem," Sin said.

"That is true. You can always count on birds to act as they are, loyal to a fault."

"I'm glad to have had you as well." Sin hugged herself, inhaling deeply, her eyes moving over the houses below to the forge behind them, finally settling on the roof of the stable. "Shayfax gave birth today."

Matteo turned toward her.

Sin hesitated. It might not be the best time to ask. Someone else might claim the foal, however, if she waited too long.

"It's a boy. I delivered him all by myself. He almost died." She sucked in a breath before she continued. "I wanted to ask if I could claim him, now that I'm a Protector?"

Matteo ambled ahead of her, folding a hand behind his neck.

"You were late."

"Not really."

"I should not award you for being late."

"I wasn't late and I wasn't too early, I was just on time. Besides, didn't you punish me already by keeping me waiting."

"A Protector needs to have patience and to be on their toes." Matteo sighed and looked at her. "We cannot fail our High King or the Aradrian people. Nothing comes before your duty. You do know that?"

"Of course I know."

He exhaled heavily, his breath wafting over her face. "Very well. The foal is yours." He put a hand under his chin. "Did you name him?"

"Vilyur."

"A good name." Matteo closed his eyes briefly. "It's time. They should all be waiting in the Dragon's Den by now."

Sin fell in step as they walked further up the pathway on the mountain's ridge.

The mouth of the Den loomed before them, lit by torches on either side of the entrance. Eager voices sounded from inside.

"Good, everyone is here." Matteo nudged Sin forward.

The walls were covered in large carvings of five dragons entwined with each other, the spikes on their backs leaving straight shadows crisscrossing over the ground.

Ward sat on one of the stone feet of a dragon, and three other brand new Protectors had found similar spots to sit. One of them was Rip. She recognized the girls, too, though she didn't remember their names. They had all been given the Rite that day, however. The girls were from different houses, yet Sin had often seen them together as though they were friends, or perhaps closer than friends. She wrinkled her nose. A Protector of the Order should not have friends or otherwise, especially not another Magical.

"Sin, I would like you to meet Rip. He's a Marksman." Matteo gestured at the boy.

A Marksman. Not an uncommon skill, though fairly practical in a fight. She had two marks on her shoulders for fledglings with the same power who would never complete their training. She had completed it for them. They never even got to raise their blades.

"Hi, again," Sin said.

Rip crossed his arms and leaned against the stone

LINN TESLI

tail of a dragon. He grinned as widely as he had that morning.

Matteo folded his hands behind his back. "Good. And you already know Ward. Lacy over there." He tilted his head at one of the girls. Her hair was pink, her eyes turquoise. "Lacy is an Illusionist. Quite useful as skills go. Be careful around her, though. Things tend not to be what they seem."

Sin made a mental note not to be fooled by Lacy's tricks. An Illusionist was sure to have some. It sounded like a rather harmless power, though Sin had known one other Illusionist in the past, and the things they could spin was the kind of stuff nightmares were made of. There was plenty of situations where a skill like hers might prove useful.

The other girl had her hand on Lacy's forearm, while stroking her fingers lightly through the Illusionist's pink tresses.

"I'm Mercy," she said. Her full lips looked almost like she was smiling, though not quite, and her dark skin made her nigh on invisible when she angled into the shadows. Sin squinted. She wasn't sure how to interpret Mercy's expression.

"House of Earth, right?" Sin asked. "And what is your contribution to the team?"

Matteo leaned closer. "Venomizer."

Mercy wiggled her thick eyebrows, her moss-colored hair fanning out around her face.

Rip caught Sin's eye again. "And you. You are a Seeker."

"I am," replied Sin.

Matteo stepped further into the Den. "Your mission is not an easy task. But combined, you share strengths that should work in our favor. We have been tracking the resistance for a while. Their leader is a bit of a mystery to us. We believe he is a Magical, though we do not know who he is or what powers he possesses. What we do know is that he is becoming a danger to Aradria, to the High King Archenon, and to the Unspelled. This leader has one goal—he wants Magicals to rise to power—he wants them to be free to practice however they wish."

"He must be mad," Lacy interrupted.

"Perhaps," Matteo said. "What he is, is poisonous. He has gained a lot of followers and we need to know exactly how many and how they intend to reach their goal. Additionally, there have been an increasing amount of reports on Magicals practicing openly. You need to find out what they are planning, then you will stop it."

"We'll take care of him. A knife to the heart will stop just about anyone." Rip grinned. He unsheathed a knife from his belt, balancing it on his fingers.

"We want this to be as quiet as possible, Rip, so he is not yours to kill. Mercy will provide what is necessary to stop him, though not before Sin's say so. Her job is to identify the leader, learn his secrets and gather the information we need. Taking down just one man isn't going to be enough. As for the rest of you, your skills will help Sin complete this mission, in any way she requires." He inhaled sharply. "Five voices with equal weight will only get you in trouble. I have chosen a leader and you will all do as she says. If Sin is not around for whatever reason, Ward will be your next in command."

"But," Rip started. "What do you need from me then, if I'm not supposed to do the kill? I never miss, you know."

"You will infiltrate the group, same as Sin, and if necessary, you will end anyone who could be seen as the potential heir to the current leader of the opposition when he is gone. We want to shut them down completely. Again, however, I must stress that you do not act until Sin has completed her job and gives you the clear. Understood?"

Rip grimaced but nodded while twirling the hilt of the knife in his hand.

"And me?" Lacy adjusted the strap fastening her cloak.

"You, dear Lace, you will be a good soldier and follow the commander. I have no doubt that your illusions will come to use."

Sin surveyed her team. They were all monstrous, each in their own way. Except for maybe Ward, though he had a different skill, one that rendered Magicals powerless if he wanted. They did have enough offense and they were infiltrating a large group of unknown members of Magicals, so she guessed a little defense couldn't hurt. It made sense to include him.

"Pack what you need. You descend at first light." Matteo took Sin with him back outside.

"I want you to send me regular updates with Nefero. If you need anything, let me know. And make sure you keep the others on a tight leash. They are talented but tend to be reckless. The Unspelled are not to be harmed. Understood?"

"Yes, Master," Sin replied.

Matteo started toward the pathway, then stopped and grabbed Sin's arms, pulling her into a hug. She wasn't sure what to do, but eventually, she found her own arms wrapping around him as well.

"I will miss you when you leave," he said.

Sin hesitated. His heart beat in a slow rhythm and she relaxed, allowing herself a moment of weakness.

"And I you."

CHAPTER THREE

THE SUN WAS ALREADY SCORCHING HOT AS THE TEAM descended the ridge of the mountain. The tall gates had shut behind them and the onyx walls surrounding the castle stood like a monument at their backs. A steep stairwell guided them down the path with the least resistance, but it would be a couple of days yet before they reached the plains below.

Sin walked last, allowing her to keep an eye on her team while also having their backs, though nothing much would attack them this far up the mountain. There were a few animals further down but up here there were mostly winged creatures who kept to their own.

She tore her eyes away from what had been her home and safe place for as far back as she had memory. Instead she surveyed the mountainside of black stone. Hardly anything grew up here that one did not plant themselves. A few mountain roses would force their way through, however, adding shades of blue to the otherwise blackness.

Rip stopped to wait and fell in step with her. "Mind if I walk with you?" he asked. "The steps are wide enough here."

She glanced at the narrow stairwell and over the edge. One wrong step and it didn't matter who you were. Unless you could fly, you'd be dead.

"Sure," she said. "You take the shade. I'll walk in the sun." She had wanted to keep a safer distance from the edge, though she was team leader and part of her job was to keep her team safe. That included Rip.

"You can hold my arm if you like." Rip flashed a row of gleaming white teeth.

"I'm good as I am, thank you."

"Offer stands whenever you change your mind."

Sin frowned. Was he trying to romance her? She almost laughed. She did have eyes, and she had to admit that he was all right to look at, if one enjoyed a slightly crooked nose and stubbled cheeks. But no one could love someone like her. Not truly. She didn't even love herself. Besides, love—like pain—was weakness.

Rip angled closer to the mountainside, still smiling like an idiot. Perhaps if love wasn't an issue, there were other ways they could enjoy one another. But who had time for things like that?

"You know you're famous on Fyra, right?" Rip skipped over a broken step down the stairwell.

"Huh?"

"You have never been defeated, not once. Not in

training matches, and obviously never in a deathmatch."

"That's not true. Who in Aradria told you such a rock-headed thing?"

"Everyone says so."

"You really believe that five-year-old me was never defeated in trial combat? So many times. Matteo had me pinned for dead for years."

"Sure, but training with a Grand Master doesn't really count. Did you ever lose to an equal opponent?"

Sin wrinkled her nose. Had she? "I don't recall that I ever have."

"Exactly. You were born for this."

Sin wasn't sure what all this praise was good for, though he was right in that she was born to become a Protector, no matter what her parents might have thought about her. She felt the truth of it in her heart. This had always been her path.

"Have you ever lost a match?" Sin asked.

"Plenty." Rip retrieved a knife from his belt and flung it in the air. The knife went straight up, made a twirl and rushed straight down again before it turned and embedded itself into a large mountain snake five steps down.

"If I never miss my mark, then how am I supposed to train for a kill without the order of actually killing my opponent? I was bound to lose some. Never lost a deathmatch, though. Got the marks to prove it."

"Poor excuse." Sin hopped down the steps and crouched to pick up the lifeless snake. The silver and sapphire-colored scales were vibrant. She pulled the knife out, handing it back to Rip, before she placed the snake on a slab of stone, rolling it into a spiral. She looked around until her eyes settled on a turquoise mountain rose nearby. She picked it, careful not to pull its roots out, and laid it in the middle of the hooped body of the snake.

"We should eat it," Rip said.

"We will. I wanted to pay respects first."

"Odd." Rip said, scratching his neck.

It was admittedly a little odd, but animals had always treated Sin with kindness. This snake would fill their bellies and it felt right to thank it somehow. Even if the snake would never know she had done so.

Lacy turned a few steps ahead of them and Mercy stopped beside her. Ward was further down still.

"We should get to the outpost before it gets dark," Lacy called. "Are you keeping pace?"

"Just catching dinner," Rip called back.

Sin dumped the snake into his arms. "You killed it, you carry it."

It would make it harder for him to balance down the steps. They couldn't leave it, however, now that it was dead and all. It was large enough to feed the entire team for at least a few days.

Rip twined the snake around his neck like a scarf until it was hanging head and tail down to his thighs.

"This has to be a good look on me!" he shouted after Sin as she rushed away to catch up with the rest of the team. She turned back for a moment to make sure he was all right and shook her head at him. That was not a good look for anyone.

They walked in silence while the sun began to set, and reached the outpost as the last rays of the evening played over the horizon.

The five of them dropped their belongings at the outskirts of the camp site. The ground was more level and a few spurts of green grew in patches around the site. If they kept the pace, they should reach the plains in no more than another sleep after this one.

They all collapsed to the ground.

Ward was the first to sit and he began gathering wood for the fire. A generous pile of firewood had been stored by the Order on a carved out ledge in the mountainside. Mercy and Lacy arranged their sheepskins in the shade of an extended part of the wall of stone while Rip doused himself in the water from his waterskin.

As the fire grew, they gathered on the logs that served as benches. Rip skinned the snake, which was soon cooking on a slab of stone above the fire.

He poked the fire with a stick, a rain of embers clouding the air. "What's Ward short for anyway? I can't recall if it was mentioned during the Rite."

Ward shrugged. "Nothing. It's just Ward."

"Huh." Rip's stick caught fire and he threw it to the ground to stomp on it.

Lacy stretched herself. "Ha! That's a weird name. I go by Lace or Lacy."

"Which is short for?" Ward asked.

Lacy perched her lips. "Lavendeluciana."

Rip burst out laughing. "No wonder they didn't mention your full name during the Rite. I bet Matteo had no idea how to pronounce it." He dumped back on his bottom. "You really shouldn't pick on someone's name with one like yours."

Sin stared at the group of them and found herself giggling.

Lacy crossed her arms over her chest.

"I'll have you know it's a well-regarded Siren name, given only to infants with hair like mine."

Resting on his elbows, Rip grimaced. "It's still ridiculous."

Mercy took Lacy's hand. "I think it's beautiful."

The girls leaned against each other, and Lacy relaxed her posture.

"Sinyara on the other hand." Rip boasted. "Now that's a name. A great one in fact. Almost as good as Rip."

It really wasn't. Sin coughed. "What about yours, Mercy?"

The Venomizer looked up. "It's my birth name. I decided to keep it. Seems silly to change a name that befitting for an Aradrian Protector, don't you think?"

It was the perfect name for a Protector, and Sin felt a twang of shame for a name like her own. Mercy was what Protectors showed by ending lives as swiftly and painlessly as possible. They were not supposed to cause pain if they didn't have to. Sin was what they did, merely by existing. They were all sinners. Some more than others, and some, like her, had sins that could never be absolved, other than by the edge of a blade. Perhaps not even then.

Mercy and Lacy were still holding hands, their eyes glued to Ward, their bodies leaning forward.

Lacy threw her hands in the air. "Nothing."

"Give it!" Mercy grinned.

Lacy retrieved a necklace from her belongings and handed it to Mercy. It was made of obsidian stone, from Mount Fyra itself, reworked into cylinder-like pieces and threaded together with a leather band. "I thought for sure he would croak," she said.

Ward coughed, spitting water. "What?"

The necklace glimmered in the firelight as Mercy waved it in the air. "You're fine. I told Lacy you would be. Magic doesn't bite on you, so neither did the potion I slipped into your waterskin earlier. It really is fascinating, though I have no idea how that helps either of us with this mission."

Sin kicked the necklace out of Mercy's hand. She picked it up and gave it to Ward. "If anyone deserves this, it's him. We're a team and no one will attempt to kill another member of our team ever again. Understood?"

"Whatever you say." Mercy rolled her eyes. "But I won that necklace fair and square. Could I have it back now?"

"No. It's Ward's. He earned it for not dying."

Lacy giggled while Mercy sulked. They were an odd pair, and though Sin wasn't sure how Ward would be able to protect himself in combat, she knew what

Matteo had said, and the Shield undoubtedly served a purpose. Besides, he was a part of their team, and they had to stick together if they were going to execute their mission as intended.

Ward twitched. "I don't really need this. I mean, it would look a lot better on Mercy than on me."

"It's yours," Sin said sternly and watched as Ward tucked the necklace away. He had a point. What would he do with it? Wear it? But she had made a decision and she was not going to back down.

Rip poked the fire again with the remnants of the stick. "That was a cruel thing to do," he muttered. "We're supposed to take care of each other."

The girls gaped.

"Don't look at me like that. I'm counting on each of you to have my back when the time comes. We are Protectors now, and we protect. That is what we do. We can't do that if we attack another Protector."

Sin offered him a smile. It was the most sensible thing he had said for the short time she had known him. Perhaps there was more to him than she had thought.

Rip retrieved a whetstone from his haversack. It was a hexagon shape of white quartz and limestone. He drew his knife from its scabbard, poured some water from his waterskin onto the stone and began whetting the blade.

The girls ignored him and Mercy began braiding Lacy's hair, her gaze on Ward. "How does it work exactly?"

"What?" Ward stared at the flames.

"I mean, if you absorb our powers, or I don't know what you do, but does that mean we can't use ours around you at all?"

"I can choose to impair anyone within my range of sight. It will often happen on its own, though, if people are standing close enough. But touch will always render a Magical powerless."

"Please don't ever touch me," Mercy said, tugging at Lacy's hair.

"Ouch," Lacy uttered.

"Why would I?" Ward asked.

Sin bit the inside of her cheek. Ward's power could definitely be of some use, though it seemed like it might also be a hinderance. Mercy had a valid point.

"How are we supposed to fight if we lose our powers around you?" Sin asked.

Ward held his index finger in the air. "Master Kantos gave me something for that." He stood and took his shirt off.

"What are we looking at here?" Rip teased.

"The breastplate." Ward pointed at his chest. "Master Kantos says my magic is tied to my heart. This prevents it from affecting anyone without me intending to. It still doesn't stop it when I touch someone, though."

"Huh." Rip put his whetstone away and pulled free a piece of snake meat with his teeth.

"I always thought magic sat in the brain?" Lacy tapped her head.

"You'd need a brain for that." Rip laughed with his mouth full.

Lacy's hair was done and she helped herself to a piece of the snake. "I'll get you back for that, Marksman." Her voice was soft like velvet, though she sounded more like the snake she bit into once had.

"If everyone is done," Sin interrupted. It was time to stop the conversation before they began attacking each other again. "We need to sleep. We'll move again at first light."

In not long, they would all turn in for the night. Sin watched the stars for a while. They looked the same as from the window in her room at the House of Spirit. There was no way to tell they were any further away here than they were there.

"Got room?" Rip stood by her side with a sheepskin tucked in his arms. "The girls are making too much noise. And Ward snores."

Sin closed her eyes and said nothing.

"I know you're awake. I saw your eyes close."

"Go on, then. There's space next to me. Though I warn you, I might snore, too."

"Your snores I think I can handle. Ward sounds like a panting ox. Who would've thought? He's so scraggy."

Sin yawned. "Be nice to him."

"I am. Those girls, however."

Sin shut her eyes again, trying to find sleep for real this time. The sound of Rip's breath was making it difficult. He was moving closer. The warmth of his hand touched her just before he did. He laced his fingers with hers and her heart bounced in her chest. She wasn't sure what to do about this. Should she let him hold her hand? It would be easier to pull away and she had not invited this handhold-ing. She grunted and turned her back on him, his fingers sliding out of hers. Relaxing, she drifted off to sleep.

Rip's agonized scream forced Sin awake again. She sat abruptly, turning her head this way and that.

"What's going on."

There was no reply. Rip sat on his knees, shaking his head, still screaming. Apart from his loud shouting, there were no other sounds that didn't belong. Some-thing was definitely amiss but she couldn't spot any immediate danger.

Lacy leaned against the mountain wall behind Rip. Was she smirking?

He reached out and patted the sheepskin next to Sin. "Who did this to you?" he howled.

"Did what?"

"If it was one of those mischievous skanks, I'll throw my knife at their hearts without blinking."

Lacy laughed, her voice echoing in the night.

"What did you do?" Sin yelled at her.

The Illusionist shrugged, snapped her fingers and walked off.

This had to stop. Sin grabbed Rip's shoulders and shook him hard until the screaming subsided.

"Sin?" he asked.

"What happened?"

"You were dead. Your brains were everywhere. I... what...?"

Sin scowled in the direction of Lacy, then locked eyes with Rip. "It was an illusion. I know she said she would get back at you, but I had no idea this would be how or I would have ordered her to back off on torment as well as death."

"An illusion?" Rip shook his head, his body relaxing slightly. "Such a skank. Bloody insane power, though."

Sin nodded. It was cruel and more than a little dangerous. Once their mission was over she would have to consider reporting Lacy as a magical danger to Aradria. If taken seriously, the Grand Masters would have her executed, so Sin would not decide before she had seen the girl in combat.

"She's gone. Go back to sleep now," Sin shushed.

Rip tilted his head down, his eyes still raised to hers.

"Can I hold you when we sleep?"

"You don't rest, do you? Even now?"

"I thought you were dead. I don't want either of us to die and never have held you first."

Sin sighed. "At least you asked me first this time. You can hold my hand. But that's all."

"I'll take it." He clasped her hand and they lay back down. His palm was moist and warm, and the sound of his breath was heavy in her ears. Sin tried to ignore him. She would have to find a way to keep her team from tearing each other apart. Perhaps when they found the opposition and their goal was made clear, they could turn their focus on their common enemy. But it was still a while before they reached the city. Luckily, they would find another mode of transportation at the foothills of the mountain. The horse mistress Yirin would hopefully have the unicorns ready for them when they got there. Getting off their feet for a while might just keep them all in better spirits.

CHAPTER FOUR

SIN HOPPED OFF THE LAST STONE SHELF, DROPPING DOWN to plant her feet steadily on the soil of the Caradrean plains. The air was dry, the minuscule grains and dust scraped against her skin. The scent of sage tickled her nose. She pulled her scarf up to shield more of her face.

"There!" Ward said as he jumped to the ground next to her.

Sin shifted her eyes. Only about a hundred steps further south along the foothills was a stable, a barn and a small farmhouse. That would be their next stop.

Rip, Lacy and Mercy hit the ground next to them, and they moved forward.

Sin looked around. The area was quiet, no one was outside besides a few sheep and a rooster. The bird cocked his head at them as they turned the corner of the farmhouse. Its feathers rustled and it blew its chest out.

"Easy," Rip said. "Or I'll have you for dinner."

The rooster cocked its head to the other side then turned its back on them and wobbled into the barn.

"You think anyone is home?" Lacy asked, dusting herself off to no use.

"One way to find out." Sin turned to the farmhouse when something caught her attention. She spun on her toes, crouching.

"What?" Rip asked.

"There are Magicals here." She angled her head and looked for any signs of what she'd sensed. "There." She pointed at the stable. "There's something going on in there."

"How many?" Mercy asked.

Sin couldn't be sure. It wasn't an exact science. But there was at least two Magicals inside. Maybe more.

A wild elf came running out from behind the stable with a finger over her mouth. She waved at them to come closer. She wore an apron over what looked like garments made from nothing but roots and leaves, clinging to her dark skin. Twigs and vines held her raven-black hair away from her face, creating a crown on her head.

Sin gestured for the others to follow. They were all alert, taking soft steps as they approached the elf.

"You have to help them," the elf said.

"Who are you?" Ward asked.

"The name is Yirin. I manage this place. The Protectors were only returning the unicorns..." She shifted her eyes, her sinuous body rigid and as alert as the rest of them. "...There were four of them that I could tell.

The attackers. I don't know if there are any others with them."

Sin shook her head in disbelief. "Why are they attacking Protectors? Are they Magicals too?"

"I don't know. I didn't see them perform any magic. I was in the back stall when it happened and slipped out the back door before they could see me."

"All right. We'll help." They couldn't very well allow an attack on fellow Protectors.

"Lace, Mercy. Go with Yirin through the back. It might give us an edge of surprise. Boys, you're with me." She glanced at Ward. "Are you up for this?"

He had a slight tremble on his lips but his eyes were clear and his brows gave a dip towards the ridge of his nose. He was determined if nothing else.

"I'll do my best," he said.

"Don't worry." Rip slapped a hand on his back, forcing Ward to expel air. "We'll protect you."

Sin narrowed her eyes to slits and Rip held his palms up. "Let's do this."

The stable doors were already open, dust blowing inside and clouding their vision as it entered the streaks of sunlight. Sin drew her sword and stepped into the stable, quickly assessing the situation.

Two people hung by their feet from a beam under the ceiling, the mark of the dragon visible on one of their bare shoulders. Their arms and legs were bound and their mouths covered shut. A couple of Unspelled stood underneath them, and a Magical sat on a ball of hay by a nearby stall. Sin glimpsed the girls and the elf hiding in the back stall. The Unspelled would be easily dealt with. The Magical, however. What was he?

"You take those two," Sin pointed with her sword. "No magic." She swung her blade again. "That one ... Magical. He's mine."

The strangers' eyes fell on Sin and the boys, and the Magical leaped to his feet. Sin could almost taste it as the magic built around him, snaking out around his body. A vivid shade of teal intensified around his neck.

"Cover your ears," Sin yelled. "He's going to scream."

Sin grabbed two handfuls of muck and stuck it in her ears just as the man released his scream. She glanced at the boys as Rip fell to his knees, his hands flying up over his ears. It wouldn't be enough. A few drops of blood trickled out underneath his hands. She sensed it, too, though it was more like a loud, shrieking whistle. Ward shrugged and Sin waved at him to keep going. The magic didn't affect him. It did, however, affect Rip and likely the rest of her team hiding in the back stall.

"Stop," she cried out. "You're killing them."

A woman stepped out of a stall to Sin's right. Heavy boots accompanied tight leggings and a black tunic. Her hair was braided tight to her scalp, trailing over her head and down her back. The muscles on her body bulged and gave her a masculine appearance. "That would be the intention," she mouthed. Sin's days of studying lip reading came in handy because she couldn't hear anything but the whistle in her head.

She screamed back, releasing her most feral war cry before she charged forward. It was like running against the tide, like waves crashing into her to try and wash her backward. The blood thinned in her veins and her airways clogged. It was as if her bones tried to wring themselves from their sockets.

"Stop it!" she cried again, though she wasn't sure if any sound came out.

She gathered all her strength and lunged forward.

The screaming man's eyes widened as she came at him. She drove her sword into his mouth, piercing the top of his head. The whistle stopped and she filled her lungs with air before it was pushed right back out. A brutal force slammed against her spine and sent her staggering forward.

She rolled aside. A fist hit the ground next to her head. Sin kicked the woman in the stomach. Her foot shook at the impact. It felt like kicking a rock. Her opponent wasn't a Magical but she was extremely well trained. The woman straddled Sin and went for another blow. The taste of iron filled Sin's mouth, her arms firmly locked to her sides by her opponent's knees.

The woman's arm came swinging again and Sin tensed, awaiting the hit. A spray of blood washed over Sin's face before the woman's arm thumped down beside her before the rest of her toppled off Sin, her hand fumbling over the open wound on her shoulder where her arm had been attached.

Ward stood behind her. He shook, his face and

clothes drenched in blood. He dropped his sword, shaking his head.

Sin nodded at him in approval and found her footing while digging the muck from her ears. The woman would bleed out soon, and was no longer a threat. Neither was the Screamer. She shifted her gaze. The elf was busy calming the unicorns and ignoring everything else. Mercy and Lacy sat on top of the bodies of the two Unspelled. They had been clean kills, though Sin was less than pleased that they'd killed Unspelled when instructions clearly stated that they weren't supposed to. Circumstances forced their hands, however. Sin would let this one slide.

"Ugh." Rip's voice caught Sin's attention and she ran over to him.

"Are you all right?"

"It felt like my head was about to explode. I think it would have, too, if that infernal noise had gone on for much longer." He took her hand and she pulled him to his feet. "I guess I owe you one."

"I couldn't very well let you die. Where would I get my entertainment then?"

She smiled at him and cringed. Her cheek was swollen. They rolled a couple of balls of hay underneath the Protectors still hanging from the ceiling before Lacy and Ward cut them down.

"How come you guys weren't affected by the Screamer?" Rip asked the girls.

"I don't know. Perhaps because he wasn't targeting

us?" Mercy said. "He only saw you. So when Sin shut him up, we went for those Unspelled dimwits."

"They didn't even see us coming." Lacy winked.

Sin helped remove the ropes on the Protector's arms and the bonds around their mouths. Her eyesight blurred slightly on the left side and she blinked hard. It was a woman and a man, only a couple of years older than Sin.

"Thank you," the man said.

"Everett?" Sin smiled. It hurt this time.

"Sinyara!"

She bumped her fist on his shoulder. Everett was from her house. His chin was broader then she remembered. As were his shoulders.

"I haven't seen you since the Rite two years ago."

"We've kept busy. That's Aisla. We're the last members of our team."

The last? Sin's heart dropped. "I'm terribly sorry." She sat on the ball of hay next to him. "What happened to you?"

"The first year went pretty well. We completed our missions and everything was fine. This past year, however, things have gotten weird. We've been attacked numerous times. By people like the ones you took out here. They tend to be a mix of Magicals and Unspelled for some reason, though I have no idea why they're attacking us."

Lacy shook her hair and crouched in front of him. "You've got a nasty cut on your chin," she said, pushing Sin to the side. "Allow me to clean it for you. And Sin, you should duck yourself in a trough. You look like you've just stepped out of a rainfall of blood. That cheek could use some ice, too, though I'm not sure where you'd get some of that. Water will have to do."

Sin wiped her forehead, the moisture sticking both ways to her skin. Lacy was right.

"You guys can clean in here while Ward and I wash up."

Sin dragged Ward with her outside and found a trough full of water where they could wash. He looked about as bad as she assumed she did. The water went from slightly brown to muddy and red as they washed. A radiating pain shot through her spine each time she bent forward. Meanwhile the others were piling the bodies up outside.

Ward stuck a hand inside a pouch in his belt and retrieved a vial. He dripped two drops on his tongue and put it back.

"What's that?" Sin tilted her chin at the pouch.

"Master Kantos started giving these to me years ago. It helps channel my powers, gives me more focus."

Mercy stood by the stable doors with the dead woman's arm in her hands, leaning into the sun. "What's it of?"

"A mixture of Sandman root, elfen berries and leaves from a midnight rose," Ward replied.

Mercy shook her head. "That won't do shit to help you channel shit. If anything, it will inhibit your power."

"You're wrong," Ward said. "I can control who to target and who not to now."

"If you say so. Perhaps Kantos thought your power was too nefarious for you to have the full use of it? I mean, a mixture and a breast plate? But what do I know, huh? I only specialise in herbs and potions." She chucked the arm on top of one of the bodies then turned on her heels and stepped back inside.

Sin raised an eyebrow. If anyone knew about remedies and mixtures, it was the Venomizer. And if Mercy was right, it would mean that Ward's power was considered dangerous enough that it needed to be contained.

"Master Kantos must have good reason for wanting you to take this mixture. I have complete faith that he knows what he's doing."

Ward took a couple of swigs from his water skin. "Not to worry. I'm not about to let Mercy mess with my head."

"Good," Sin said. "And thanks for saving my life back there."

"I almost didn't." He stared at his feet. "I mean, I hesitated, wasn't sure what to do. But when her arm went up, I swung my blade as hard as I could. It was luck more than anything else."

"Well, then. We're going to have to practice your combat skills. One hour every day from now on."

Ward smiled. "Yes, Commander. I'd like that."

They were about finished washing up when the wild elf came outside.

"You have my gratitude," Yirin said. "Grand Master Matteo already sent word you would come, so your unicorns are ready when you are. You may stay the night, however. It's the least I can offer."

"Appreciated," Sin replied, eyeing the dead. "What do you want us to do with them?"

"I'd say we burn them. They don't deserve to return to Aradrian soil."

It was settled. The team, Everett, and Aisla, made sure the bodies were far enough from the farm before they torched them. The Protectors they had saved would not stay, however. They would continue their ascent up Mount Fyra as planned.

The air filled with ash that the wind carried out across the plains as the two Protectors walked away. While the bodies burned, Sin's team helped Yirin clean the stables of blood and tend to the unicorns before they finally found the beds she had offered. Sin twisted and turned the entire night. Something was wrong and she couldn't figure out what. Magicals and Unspelled together, attacking Protectors. They would have to watch their backs going forward. Something was clearly very wrong.

CHAPTER FIVE

GRAINS OF SAND WHIPPED AROUND THEM AS THE UNICORNS sped across the plains. The wind had picked up over the course of the day, and the sandstorm was now at full force. There was no place to take shelter on the plains, though, so the team pushed on.

"I can't see shit," Rip called. "Time to camp, Commander?"

Sin frowned. The storm made it impossible to tell the direction, but she didn't want to stop. Rip was right, however. All she saw was dust and sand. There was no point in continuing while the storm raged.

"Halt!" Sin yelled. The wind whined, muffling her voice. She wasn't sure if they could all hear her. "Is everyone here?"

Something whirled past her and a zinging noise pierced the whooshing sounds of the storm.

A sudden jolt to her chest sent her flying off the unicorn. She landed with a heavy thud, grasping at what it was that had hit her. Her fingers traced the smooth surface with rough ridges before gliding over an elongated part of the skull of what had likely been a small Vulkan Eagle. She folded her hand around it and pushed herself up by her palms. Tiny splinters of bone pierced her skin as the skull cracked under her weight. She fell to her stomach, feeling the ground with her fingertips as she crawled forward.

"Rip?" she called against the wind. All she could hear was the storm screeching back. "Ward? Anyone?"

The grains clawed at her skin as the sand crept under the seams of her garments. She shook herself and held her arms up, shielding her eyes as she sat on her knees. There was no use moving further. She was completely blind against the forces of nature. The beat of her pulse quickened, and she felt a twinge in her thigh as the bindings no doubt had opened up again.

A shadow moved within the dreadful sheets, growing increasingly closer. Sin let out a sigh of relief.

"We're here," Mercy and Lacy called as they trotted towards her.

"Us too." Rip and Ward emerged at Sin's side.

Sin fell back, sprawling on the ground.

Rip extended his hand and drew her with him to the animals. The team slid off their unicorns, leaving them standing in a semicircle against the wind. Their large bodies provided a modest shelter from the screeching gusts and they were more accustomed to the plains than the team was.

"Closer," Sin croaked.

The team sat and huddled close to the magical creatures at their backs.

"Cover your faces as much as you can." Sin pulled her hood further down over her eyes, then held her cloak firmly around herself. She squinted through the dust clouding her vision to find the others doing the same. There was nothing to do but wait it out. At least they were all in the same spot.

A hand slid over her aching back as Rip idled closer.

"I got you," he said. His voice sounded like he was much further away than he was.

She let him hold her. It was better to sit close than apart as the wind tore at them.

They sat like that while the storm screeched. The darkness grew and Sin buried her face between her knees. She coughed, pressing her eyes shut. She had no idea how long they had been sitting there when the wind began to still.

"Hey," Rip whispered. "Sin."

She looked up into Rip's amber eyes. Her vision blurred but she could see him.

"It's passed."

The storm had ended quicker than it had begun. Sin exhaled heavily, removing her hood. She coughed again and brushed her palms over her face. It stung like she had been bitten by a swarm of wasps.

A sheet of sand blew over the ground where a large scorpion had hidden. The creature lifted its tail and zigzagged around itself before it scurried for cover under a nearby rock. The last wisps of dust disappeared across the ground and the sky was lit by twinkling stars.

"Is everyone all right?" Sin asked.

"A few scratches, is all," Rip replied.

Lacy was in Mercy's arms and Ward was still hugging himself. They were covered in dust and scratches, lines of red painting their faces.

Lacy slid her hands into her hair and shook it, spraying dust all over Mercy. It didn't make much difference as she was already covered in sand. "We should make a fire and wash."

"On it." Rip bounced to his feet and went to his unicorn to retrieve a few logs of firewood hanging from one of the bags fastened on the steed's back.

The boys got the fire started and a kettle of water soon simmered above the flames.

"Here." Ward held up a piece of cloth in front of Sin's face. "Allow me?"

She leaned away from him for a moment. What was he doing?

"It will sting, but it needs to be cleaned," Ward said.

She glanced at Rip, who was watching her with his arms crossed over his chest. She inhaled sharply and motioned forward. "All right then. Easy, though."

Ward nodded and carefully touched the cloth to her skin. He'd been right. It did sting. He soaked the cloth again, wrung it and repeated the process a number of times. "There," he said.

"Appreciate it."

A knife blurred past Sin's vision and she glared at Rip.

"Got to eat," he said, bouncing to his feet. He retrieved the knife and the Caradrean scorpion it was embedded into. The scorpion was the size of a large rat. It wouldn't entirely fill their stomachs, and scorpions tasted like stale bread. It was still food, however.

"I'll cook it," Mercy said, sliding it off the blade with two fingers. She broke off the tip of its tail and put it into one of her many pouches.

Sin thanked Ward again, then went to sit with Rip. She grabbed a piece of cloth, dipped it in some water and tilted her chin at him.

"You look like you crawled through the netherworld and back," she said.

He grinned at her. "Better than usual then."

The grime on his face did little to hide the dimple on his cheek or the clarity of his gaze. Sin grimaced but began to clean his face. The sand had scraped his skin, drawing blood at will, but the cuts were thin and mostly superficial. It would heal quickly enough.

"There. Best I could do."

They nodded at each other and Sin sat back beside him.

"Food's done," Lacy announced. She sliced off a piece for each of them.

The meat resisted every bite as Sin chewed into it, but it was better than nothing. When she had no more meat left, she stood and retrieved a thin blade. This would be as good a time as any to try and get the team to bond with each other. "I think someone has earned his first mark." She gestured with the knife at Ward.

"I... uh." Ward shook his head.

"You killed my attacker, Ward. You should get a mark. Mercy and Lacy have earned a mark each, too. And so have I." She shifted her eyes to Rip. "I'm sure you'll get several more of your own once this mission is done."

He winked and shifted his whetstone between his hands.

Mercy looked up from combing Lacy's hair. "You're the only one who killed a Magical, Sin. None of us earned nothing."

"But..." Sin's shoulders slumped. Mercy was right. Again. They shouldn't earn marks for killing the Unspelled. She had wanted Ward to get his first mark so much that she hadn't even considered who it was he had killed. She wasn't sure why, but it mattered to her much more than she had thought. He had no marks at all. It would have been nice to be the one to grant him his first. Moreover, he had saved her life.

"It's all right," Ward said. "I'll mark you, though. I mean, I do owe you your thirtieth mark, as I did kind of take that away from you last time."

"Fine, then. But you'll get yours. And when you do, I'll be the one to mark your skin. Agreed?"

"Yes, Commander."

Sin pushed the cape away from her shoulder and removed her gauntlet before pulling down her sleeve and exposing her shoulder.

"You need to heat it first." She handed the knife to him and he placed it in the flames from the campfire for a while before retrieving it.

"Where do you want it?" Ward asked.

"Where there's room."

Ward straightened, then moved around Sin. The warmth from his hand clasped around her upper arm. Her thirtieth mark. It wouldn't be her last, but it did feel special. She had wanted to reach thirty for a long time, and Ward had been a disappointment that day they first met in the arena. She was glad now, however, that she hadn't killed him. And though she wanted the mark, killing was not something to celebrate. Death, however, was something to honor. The Screamer had been a Magical, a threat. She had taken away his pain, absolved him from a cruel life. He was at peace now, and could no longer hurt anyone. Killing him was a favor to both him and to the Aradrian people.

"Ready?" Ward asked.

"Go on."

The edge of the knife burned into her flesh, digging beneath her skin. The sharp pain traveled slowly across the top of her shoulder blade, and she inhaled deeply. The sensation of the burn was familiar, comforting somehow. The heat was a promise of a safer Aradria, and the pain was her remorse burning to a crisp. Ward put the blade away and rinsed the wound.

"Looks good."

Sin pulled her shirt back up and covered her shoulders with her cape again, then put her gauntlet back on.

A smile painted her face. She had gotten her thirtieth mark.

"There's room for more," she said as she fell back to rest on the sand. How many more marks she would earn by the end of this mission was unclear, though it would likely be more than a few. And she looked forward to helping guide more Magicals of Aradria toward absolution.

Rip came over to lay next to her. He rolled to his side, resting his head in his palm. "I tried counting the stars."

"I always lose track and have to start over," Sin murmured.

"My master used to tell me a story about the stars; that they were once dragons and the stars are there to remind us of them. They may be gone from the world, but we shall not forget them."

"Matteo told me that's why the Order took the name of Dragon. That when a dragon—or a Magical—dies by sacrifice, they're released from their magic and their life, so that their souls can be free and become a bright star in the sky to guide others—to be at peace."

Rip rolled his eyes. "Sounds like hogwash. Though I wouldn't mind becoming a star after this."

"It's a children's story." The touch of Rip's hand on hers made her flinch, but instead of pulling away she wrapped her fingers in his. "It's what they tell Magical children so they will think there's something better to follow the cruelty of their lives. We're not children anymore, and what we are will never qualify for eternal life as a shining star. We are not stars, we are the ashes that are left when embers die, we are the blood that flows by the edge of steel, children of shadows and terror." She inhaled sharply. "Stars are for the blessed, not the damned."

Rip's eyes widened. "That's some dark shit." He twitched his nose. "But true. I don't mind the darkness, however. Only when it gets too crowded. For you, though, I'll stay in the shadows. The sky can keep its stars."

Sin felt a tug at the corner of her mouth. There was something about him. He got her, who she was. As different as they were, they were much the same. He knew as much about being a child of the night as she did. She leaned closer, drawing in the scents of ash and leather clinging to his skin.

"You can kiss me now if you want," she said.

Rip gave her a genuine smile from ear to ear. He folded his arm around her and swiftly pulled her closer. Then he kissed her. A fiery sensation stirred in Sin's veins, crawling through her chest and down her body until her toes curled. He tasted likely as bad as she did but she didn't care what he tasted like. She wanted more of him.

A twig snapped somewhere nearby as someone fed the dying fire. Sin disengaged from Rip. She had almost forgotten that they weren't alone, and there wasn't anywhere to hide either. She sat and met Ward's stare across the flames. His gaze fell and he looked away, turning to his unicorn.

He was upset? Kissing Rip had been foolish. What was she thinking? This was hardly the best way to strengthen her team, and she couldn't make it look like she was playing favorites.

"Hey, Ward. I know it's late, but I did promise we would practice every day. We haven't had the chance with the storm and everything. What do you say?" Sin called.

Ward turned back. "It's kind of dark."

"Even better. You'll have to rely on your other senses."

He drew his sword and took a bow, smiling gently. "Promise you won't kill me?"

"I was told you're an asset, so I'll try not to." She bumped Rip on his arm and he waved at her as she sprang off. She wasn't sure why Ward looked so sad, though she was going to do the best she could to cheer him up—and perhaps gift him with a couple of bruises.

CHAPTER SIX

A<small>N</small> <small>ENORMOUS BUILDING ROSE ABOVE THE SAND DUNES,</small> five gleaming pearl-white spears twinkling in the rays from the midday sun. Nothing else was built nearby, but the city of Valano loomed close on the horizon beyond. Sin patted the silver mare she had borrowed on the neck. Even though the unicorns had made journeying the plains a lot easier, it would be a relief to get to their destination.

"What is that?" Lacy asked.

"Didn't you read about it in one of your lessons?" Rip rolled his eyes at her.

"I'm more of a doer than a reader."

Sin shook her head. "You really should read more. A Protector needs to know Aradrian history, and this is part of that."

Lacy shrugged. "Are you going to tell me what it is?"

"It's a house of worship—the White Lady," Mercy said.

"See, no books needed. All I had to do was ask."

The white towers were weirdly ominous. It was as though something stirred in the stone walls, making the ground tremor. Sin shuddered. She wanted to leave as quickly as possible. There was too much magic tied to these grounds.

Mercy slowed her unicorn and stared at the White Lady. "It used to be a place for Magicals to worship the elements and to practice their magic. It's considered magical in essence, which is why no one dares enter it anymore."

"I think it's pretty," Lacy said.

Pretty was not what came to Sin's mind. Abhorrent maybe, uncomfortable at best. Sin kicked her heels and the unicorn trotted past the house of worship, the others following close behind her. A myriad of sensations crashed inside her. The sense of powers was so strong that she had trouble focusing her eyes.

"Hiya," she called and the unicorn set off at a gallop. Sin only pulled on the reins to slow the mare down once she could no longer sense the magic.

The rest of the team caught up and Rip steered his black steed ahead of her. "You all right?"

"I'm fine," Sin snapped.

Rip grimaced and Sin stared at her hands.

"That was uncalled for. It's just that... that place gave me the jitters. Let's move forward."

Ward came to Sin's side. "We're there."

The sand dune they were on sloped down into a sea of green. Clusters of farmhouses and buildings spread out in the valley below. On the other side, the high walls of the city of Valano towered far above the rooftops, with iron gates the height of at least ten men.

"So it seems."

They trotted down the last sand dune and continued onto a pathway that soon broadened into a road wide enough for two carriages to pass each other with ease. They rode around the corner of an abandoned farm when someone yelled.

"Please!" The woman's voice was full of despair, quivering and weak.

"We only want the child." A large man surrounded by a dark red mist of magic blocked the road, along with four other cloaked Magicals. Sin tensed.

Two coachmen sat at the front of a carriage pulled by two brown horses, while a woman had her arms protectively around a child at the back, shielding his body as best she could. One of the men raised his arms and the two coachmen shot into the air. They were suspended for a moment, their arms and legs flailing wildly. The man motioned with his hands, and the coachemen's necks snapped before they crashed to the ground. Cowards, Sin thought, as a sense of shame welled up inside. She was no better than them.

"Now," the large man bellowed. "That child is coming with us. No one else needs to die."

Sin fumed. Five Magicals against a poor Unspelled

woman and her child. She could not allow this cruelty to pass.

"We're saving that child," she announced.

Mercy pulled her green hair back, fastening it tightly with a leather band. "Of course we are."

Lacy slid off her unicorn and snapped her fingers. "I'll create an illusion so the men won't see them."

Sin nodded her assent just as one of the men grabbed the woman and pulled her away from the child. She struggled, tears streaming from her eyes, but her arms slipped away from the boy and she was thrown to the ground. The man, whose magic looked like wisps of white, bent over her and sucked the air from the woman's lungs into his own until her skin shriveled and turned ashen.

"I'm sorry," Lacy said. "Illusions take some time."

"That child is out of time." Sin shook her head. "Ward, go with Rip and disable anyone you can. Take that life-sucker down first," she commanded. "Rip. Feel free to kill."

Rip grinned. He grabbed the reins on Ward's unicorn with his own and galloped forward.

"And us?" Mercy asked.

"Feel free to join in."

"This kind of fight isn't really my thing. But I'll see what I can do," Mercy said, trotting off.

"I'll keep working on the illusion." Lacy closed her eyes, her fingers moving like a spider netting her web.

Sin couldn't wait for her to figure it out. She followed the others and climbed onto the saddle. While the unicorn gained momentum, she squatted, waiting for the right time. Her body swayed with the motions of the unicorn until she was close enough. She gathered her strength and jumped over to the carriage where she landed next to the boy.

He was sobbing, curled up against a barrel.

"I'm here to help," Sin said.

The boy, perhaps nine summers old, lifted his chin. There was no mistaking his red hair and freckled skin. He was local. "They're too strong. I should go with them so they won't hurt anyone else."

"They can't have you."

Five men against one defenseless young boy. There was no way Sin would let him surrender. She tilted her head back to look for danger. One of the attackers was already dead. Ward had his hand on the leg of the man who had sucked the life out of the boy's mother. The man inhaled and nothing happened. Clearly confused, he kept trying to suck air. Still nothing. The man kicked Ward in the face, sending him flying backward. Rip swung his blade, turned on his toes and hurled the sword at the man. It cut through the air to bury itself into the life-sucker's chest.

Mercy tapped another of the Magicals on the shoulder. He turned, his eyes wide. Mercy pulled him into an embrace and landed a kiss on his lips. The man fell dead a moment later.

Sin exhaled slowly. Her team could handle themselves. She turned back to the boy as the man with the dark red magic climbed onto the carriage.

"Mind your own, bird." He licked his lips, staring at Sin. He shouldn't have called her bird. Only Matteo was allowed to call her that.

She grabbed the boy and pushed him behind her, drew her sword and invited the fight. Her mind was open. She could read his every move, sense his power in her bones. He was a Boulder. His skin would be hard as a rock, though everyone had weak spots, and Sin had fought Boulders before.

"Mercy," Sin called over her shoulder as the Boulder slammed his fist at her. She jumped sideways onto a barrel. She had seen it coming. Another fist came swinging. She dropped back down and leaped onto the rails between the back and front of the carriage before she stabbed at his ear. He turned his face at the same time, her blade crushing at the impact with his forehead.

"Unwise," he muttered.

"And your prey has gone." Sin dropped the hilt, glancing briefly at Mercy running off with the boy. Sin yelped as a sharp pain ran up the length of her left thigh.

The man smirked, holding up a dagger covered in Sin's blood. She gritted her teeth and ducked as the blade came slashing at her neck.

The carriage rocked as the man wobbled on his feet, his eyes blinking.

"Where did you go, bird?" He kept throwing punches but his vision was clearly suffering from something.

Lacy waved and showed Sin two thumbs up.

Splinters and hay whirled around them as Sin carefully avoided the man's wild punches. She jumped off the carriage behind him. The impact sent tremors through her leg. The gash was deeper than she thought. Ward came to her side and offered up his sword. His chin was badly bruised but his eyes were vivid. They nodded at each other. He touched the Boulder's right foot, rendering his magic useless, and Sin drove the blade straight up between the man's legs. Weak spot, she thought. The man convulsed once and fell on his face, the carriage cracking at the impact.

Sin withdrew the sword, wiped it on the dead Boulder's trousers, and sheathed it. The golden dagger he had used on Sin glinted on the ground, and she decided to take it. He had no use for it anymore, so she placed it in her boot. The sword wasn't a great fit for the sheath but close enough. Ward could have it back once she found a replacement. She turned her attention to the others and counted five dead attackers, three dead Unspelled, and one breathing boy sobbing in Mercy's arms.

Sin limped over to her team, who gathered around Mercy and the boy at the side of the road. Every step was like being stabbed in the leg all over again. She would have tried to hide it but the blood wasn't exactly sparse. The familiar squawk of a falcon sounded overhead, making Sin smile against the pain. That bird was never far behind.

"Well done, Lace." Sin gave her a thumbs up and

Lacy beamed with pride. There was not one new scratch on her milky-white skin. A few cuts from the sand storm was all.

"I'm sorry it took so long. Illusions need to be built. I went as fast as I could."

Rip placed a hand on Sin's shoulder, his veins blue and his knuckles bruised. "That was some decent protecting we did there." He winked.

"You were all great." Sin eased down to sit next to Mercy and the boy. "You're safe now," she whispered.

The boy looked at her again. "But... Mother!"

There was nothing they could do about his mother, though there might be a father somewhere, Sin thought.

"I wish we would have saved her, but you're safe now. What's your name and where can we take you?"

"Eamon," the boy stuttered. "My father lives in the city. In Valano."

"Good thing that's where we're headed. You can ride with me if you want?"

Eamon leaned into Mercy and she stroked his red hair.

"You want to ride with me?" she asked in a tone of voice that was unfamiliar, almost sweet.

Eamon nodded. Perhaps Sin had frightened him? He was safe, however. That was all that mattered.

"Sin!" Ward called. There was an urgency in his voice. "You have to see this." He stood over the body of one of the dead Magicals as Sin limped to his side. He pointed at the man. "Look."

Sin took a step back. The mark of the dragon on the

man's shoulder made her stomach revolt. Her knees met the ground and her hands flew to her head. "No!" she exclaimed.

Ward crouched next to her, putting his hand on her back. "I have no idea why they did this. But I've heard stories of Protectors going rogue. Magic corrupts all."

Rogue? Her team had killed five of their own, an entire team of Protectors. If indeed they had gone rogue, it meant the men were fair kills, which in turn meant that Sin and her team had done nothing wrong. If they were mistaken, however, her and her team would become the rogue ones.

Nefero swooped by and gained height. It was a blessing that he had no voice because there was no way Sin was going to report this to Matteo. Not yet, at least.

"We need to hide the bodies. Bury them some-where," said Sin.

Ward nodded. "The farm looks empty."

Rip came to stand next to them, his hand under-neath his chin. "We could simply burn them in the barn. There's no livestock and not a person in sight. It doesn't look like anyone has lived here for some time."

Sin agreed. "Let's do that, then."

"What about her?" Ward asked, pointing at Eamon's mother.

"I don't think we should burn her with the others and we can't very well bring a body to the gates of Valano."

There was one place Sin could think of, though she did not want to go back.

73

Mercy looked at her like she knew what she was thinking. "I'll take Lace and Eamon, and we'll bury her underneath the dunes near the White Lady. We'll catch up. Meanwhile, eat this."

Mercy handed Sin a couple of leaves of some kind, which Sin didn't recognize. She narrowed her eyes, and Mercy placed her hands on her hips. "It will lessen the pain, is all. You'll feel it again in the morning, though."

Could Sin trust Mercy on this? She hesitated and searched the Venomizer's eyes. There were no signs of foul play, nothing to indicate she was lying. There was only one way to find out, and she had to be able to trust her team. Sin stuffed the leaves into her mouth and swallowed.

"All right. Do be quick. And thank you."

"The boy needs to say goodbye. But I'll make sure we don't linger."

Whatever Mercy had given Sin numbed her senses, but it helped. She bound her leg before she helped Rip and Ward carry the men into the barn after the others had left. They needed all three of them to carry the Boulder, and even then they struggled.

"I smell like a pig," Rip said, sniffing his armpit after the last of the men were finally inside.

"We all do," Ward said.

"I don't know." Sin pushed the boys amicably on their shoulders. "Pigs smell better than either of you."

They lit a fire of the dead—for the second time in only days—and walked back outside as the sun was about to set, and the chills of night drifted over Sin's skin. It would be as cold in the night as it was hot during the day this close to the plains. Sounds of crackling wood and roaring fire filled the growing darkness, casting a shimmer of orange light into the sky. They watched as the fire worked to swallow both men and barn.

The others returned before it was over, and the team turned away from their sins.

CHAPTER SEVEN

THE UNICORNS' HOOFS TAPPED RHYTHMICALLY AGAINST THE wooden surface toward the gatehouse of the city of Valano.

Sin's mare kicked a couple of stones off the drawbridge, sending them splashing into the clear water below. The moat went all the way around the outside gates to run into the ocean on the far side of the city.

A stream of fish rushed forward beneath the crystal clear water, followed by a sharp fin cutting through the surface. Sin marveled at the sight of the Venatorfish. She had read that they were the length of three men. This one was the equivalent of at least four, however. Its silver skin was inviting, the fin on its back a warning. It dipped down, its shadow disappearing as it sailed off with great speed. It was a true hunter. It takes one to know one, she thought, smiling grimly at herself and the similarities she felt toward an ocean predator.

Rip rode ahead and knocked on the gate.

"Names and business," a hoarse female voice called from the other side.

Sin dug into her haversack and found a scroll from Matteo. "We have papers."

A hatch opened further to the side.

"Leave it there," the woman croaked.

Sin placed the scroll into the hatch and it was snatched away a moment later. The team posed as gem traders. Caradreans were especially fond of all things shiny, so it made for a good cover.

The hinges creaked as the gate wheels turned and four sets of massive chains pulled the gate open enough for one unicorn and rider to enter at a time. Once the entire team was inside, the heavy gate fell thundering to the ground behind them.

"Welcome to Valano," the female voice said.

Sin looked down. A small creature with a long, crooked nose and moss-covered skin leered up at her.

"Thank you," Sin said.

It wasn't a surprise to find a Jotter at the gates of Valano, though Sin had only ever met a couple of their kin in the past. They went wherever they saw an opportunity for wealth, and Valano was one of the wealthiest cities in all of Aradria due to the amounts of gemstones they could mine. Sin had studied Valano with great interest during her geography lessons on Fyra. Healthy veins of diamonds and sapphires ran below the city through the part of Mount Fyra that stretched underground all the way from the mountain itself and into the earth below Valano, continuing into the ocean beyond.

"Rough weather these past few days," the Jotter said, eyeing the state of the team.

Sin nodded, then turned to Mercy and Eamon. "Where do you live?"

"An area called Copper Side."

"Could you point us in the direction of Copper Side, please?" Sin asked the Jotter.

The creature pointed a twisted finger with wood-like nails north, up to a winding, cobbled street between black and gold houses.

The group turned up the road and Sin took the time to soak it all in. The city smelled of soap and freshly baked bread. The houses ranged from gold to bronze and silver hues by the shimmer of the metal veins in the stone walls. There were houses here with three, four and even five stories, which appeared to be ordinary homes. The road eventually led them into an open square filled with booths and chatter issuing from a myriad of people who looked like they came from all over Aradria.

"What happens here?" Sin asked Eamon.

"Tomorrow is market day. My father will be telling tales. He's a storyteller. Mother will be trad..." His voice trailed off.

Mercy gave him a hug. "Your father will be so happy to see you," she said.

"Which way?" Sin surveyed the number of entry points to the square.

"Next left." Eamon pointed up the nearest street.

The group turned away from the square into a street of one-story buildings of black stone and copper.

"Here," the boy said. Mercy helped him down and dismounted her unicorn.

The soles of Sin's feet ached as she landed on the cobbles. She adjusted her cloak, then went to knock on the door.

"A moment," a man's voice issued from inside. The sound of shuffling paper was undeniable. Something like the turn of a key clicked before the door slid open.

The man's wrinkled face was blotched, his hair pulled back in a ponytail, and his eyes were distant, almost as white as his tresses. He leaned both hands on a twisted walking stick of red wood.

"How may I help you?" he asked.

Mercy carefully nudged the boy forward.

"Father!" the boy cried and the man's face lit up.

"Eamon!"

The boy threw himself into his father's arms and they both started weeping.

Sin frowned. Shades of marigold surrounded the man. The father was a Magical. That made no sense at all. She remembered what Everett had said, however. Magicals and Unspelled were collaborating, and though Eamon and his father were family, something felt wrong about the whole situation.

"My sweet boy." The man raised his head, his eyes flickering. "Please, come inside."

Sin looked back at her team. She hesitated but they

had come this far, and she wanted to make sure Eamon was safe. Magical father or not.

"Wait for me here."

"I'll wait outside, too," Mercy said. "I hate good-byes. It was nice to meet you, Eamon." She waved and Eamon waved back, one arm still wrapped around his father's waist.

The three of them walked inside the quaint home. It was sparsely furnished, only a table, a desk, and four chairs accompanied a worn bookshelf and a couple of large wood coffers. A woolen brown throw separated the room from the rest of the house. She inhaled and the scent of herbs and charcoal crawled up her nose.

The man gestured at one of the chairs with his walking stick. "Please sit. My name is Walis, and I thank you for bringing me my boy."

The house looked safe enough and she took the chair closest to the exit with nothing but a wall at her back and the door close by. She met the man's distant eyes.

"Whom am I speaking to?" he asked.

"The name is Sinyara. My friends and I are gem traders and we came upon your wife and son under attack."

Eamon pulled at Walis's shirt. "She fought off a Boulder to save me, Father. Can you imagine?"

"Hardly. That's mighty impressive."

Sin twined her fingers in her lap. "I'm terribly sorry but your wife... she didn't make it."

Walis pulled his fingers through his son's hair. His

lips quavered but his voice was steady. "Can you please go into the next room for a while? I would like to speak to your rescuer alone."

"All right, Father." Eamon scurried off, happier than he had been since Sin and her team found him.

"Now." Walis folded his hands in his lap. "That woman was not my wife, though she was a dear friend and I asked Eamon to call her mother. It seemed like a good idea at the time. I'm sorry if that caused you any extra concern." Walis faced Sin, a tear falling from the brim of his eye. His gaze, however, was looking toward the door. "I needed a cover. My son could not be seen outside of the city with me. I had thought they would be safe like this."

"Perhaps you should have thought to have someone abler along to protect him." It was a crass thing to say, though what he had done was foolish. Especially knowing there were people who wanted to harm his son.

"You're right. I should have taken better care, but someone more able-bodied would have been suspicious."

"Where's his real mother then?"

"She has been dead for nine summers. She died in childbirth." Walis shifted his weight. "I cannot keep him here." He breathed deeply, his body relaxing, though the sadness was all over his face. "They will come looking. I do know of a safe place where he can go, but I do not dare take him there myself for fear someone will see us together. It's where he was meant to be going when you saved him."

"You want us to take him?"

"That would be most kind. And probably a lot safer. I realize you have other business to take care of while in the city. I'm asking all the same."

"You don't know us." Sin was on edge. He was a Magical, and he was asking for help on behalf of his Unspelled son.

"No. You saved my son's life, however, so you have already earned my trust. And there are those out there that mean him harm. I'm part of a... community... of sorts. And based on what my son told me, I'd venture a guess that things did not go down entirely according to normal human potential."

Sin grimaced. He knew she was a Magical, like him, and the truth of that shared strength—or weakness—somehow made him believe they shared a bond.

"I'd rather not talk about that."

"I understand. Trust me, I do. Forgive me for my forwardness, but there are places where your magic will be accepted."

Sin's breath caught in her throat. Was this happening? Had she really stumbled upon a clue to the resistance and their whereabouts?

"Practicing magic is forbidden," she said.

"It's a shame that some believe all magic is created to cause harm when it can do so much good. Being different does not equate with being wrong."

Sin wanted to protest but it wasn't going to get her what she needed.

"We'll bring the boy with us." It wasn't favorable. Still, it might be what they had to do for their mission to succeed. Then perhaps Matteo might look the other way when he found out about what had happened with the Protectors that Sin and her team had torched.

"I'll need to make some arrangements," Walis said. "Come see me at the market tomorrow and I'll tell you where to go. Don't bring Eamon. Too many Silverlings in the city these days." Walis straightened, wiped his teary eyes, and called for his son again.

Eamon entered the room and Sin stood.

"Go with her," Walis said. "I'll see you soon."

"I don't want to leave again." The boy teared up.

"I know you don't, but we will be together again soon. Sinyara has promised to keep you safe. I think we can trust her." They hugged and Eamon followed Sin back outside.

The team sat with their backs against the house, chatting.

"I found a clue," Sin said.

"I found a tavern. If you can call it that," Ward replied.

Mercy smiled. "Why is Eamon back?"

"He still needs our help. For now, he's coming with us."

Mercy sauntered over to Eamon, offering him a hand. He took it and together they found Mercy's mare.

"Where's this tavern?" Sin opened her arms. "I think we could all use the rest."

"I'll show you," Ward said.

Eamon got back on the unicorn with Mercy and Sin mounted her own mare, following Ward and the others down an adjourning road until they reached a four-story building with a golden sign which spelled 'The Golden Chalice.'

Ward steered his mare away from the entrance. "There's a stable at the back. I'll take the unicorns there while you make arrangements with the keeper. We already made a deal regarding the unicorns. They close the entrance off at night, so they should be safe. Mercy and Eamon can help me unsaddle them and get them sorted."

"Very well," Sin said. She would rather have stayed with the unicorns, and the thought of Vilyur back at Mount Fyra passed through her mind. Being a team leader, however, meant she had to take charge and make the necessary arrangements with the keeper of the place.

Ward, Mercy, and Eamon took the unicorns with them while Rip and Lacy followed Sin inside.

The black stone interior was illuminated by the vast amount of gold covering most of the surfaces, from the table tops to the countertop of the wide bar. The few guests consisted of men and women with elaborate robes and neatly groomed hair. There was even a stage, though it was probably too late for any entertainment that night.

Lacy frantically pulled her fingers through her pink tresses. "I'm not dressed for this."

Sin crossed her arms over her chest. "You're right. We stick out like drops of blood in a cup of milk."

"Come on." Rip took both of their arms. "They have beds, and we can pay."

"Sure, but a place like this will empty our pockets pretty quickly. One night, then we find other accommodation."

"Done." Rip grinned and they approached the bar.

A Jotter dressed in a silver and gold laced midnight-blue robe greeted them on the other side of the counter-top. He was standing on a stool, pouring wine into a couple of mugs.

"I have prepared a room for you," he said, not looking at them. "There is only the one room but I've had a couple of extra beds put in, four in total. We're quite full tonight."

"We only need the one room, but we have added one more person to the list, so there's six of us." Sin put a bag of coins on the countertop.

The Jotter gave her a sideways glance. "I'm out of beds." He snatched the bag of coins away and Rip slapped his hand on the counter.

"We can manage."

They would have to. Either way, it was better than sleeping out on the plains and worrying about sand-storms. Someone had to sleep in the same bed or on the floor, though. Mercy and Lacy would be fine with one bed to share. Eamon should have his own bed, and the boys, too. Sin accepted that the floor would be her bed for their stay at the Golden Chalice.

Once everyone had settled in for the night, Sin could finally take the time to relax. The room was spacious, though the four beds made it feel more crowded. She arranged her sheepskin underneath the window to offer a view of the sky when Ward began snoring. Rip was right. He did sound like a panting ox.

A low squawk sounded outside as Nefero came to settle on the windowsill. Sin reached into her satchel and found a handful of seeds, which she placed in front of the falcon. Matteo would be expecting a report soon. The Protectors they had saved would have already told the masters of what went down at Yirin's stables, though Matteo would want to hear it from her. She yawned. It would have to wait until morning.

She had listened to the sound of her sleeping team for a while when Rip leaned over the edge of the bed closest to her. "We've slept on the ground for days. You're more than welcome to share my bed."

She offered him a smile. "No, thank you. I'm good."

"Then perhaps you would like to trade?"

"You can have it. I've got a clear view of the stars from here."

Rip dipped his head closer. "I want to kiss you again."

There hadn't been time to talk to him about her decision regarding their kiss. She wanted it, too, though not more than she wanted to keep her team strong and complete their mission.

"It's a distraction," she said.

"All right then. Let me know when you change your mind."

"I won't."

He shrugged and lifted himself further away from her, then lingered at the edge of the mattress.

"You did good today," he whispered.

"So did you."

Sin sighed. She had done good, hadn't she? They had all acted like the Protectors they were supposed to be. Lacy had proven herself to be quite valuable too, even if her powers took some time to manifest. Sin felt better about her team than she had done since they had been paired up. It took a while but sleep finally found her.

CHAPTER EIGHT

THE MARKET BUZZED WITH LIFE. ROWS OF BOOTHS AND A throng of people filled the square from one end to the other. The strong scents of meat and ale blended with a variety of herbs and spices in the air. Creatures and humans alike smiled at each other and made conversations. The laughter and distant music made the day brighter than it already was.

Sin rubbed her aching thigh as she looked around for a blacksmith. She had promised Ward they would train every day, but they should have their own swords, and she was currently hanging on to his. He wouldn't accept it back, so that morning she had used his sword while he had borrowed Rip's, and they had trained in the stables behind the Golden Chalice. So far, she had seen no swords or knives of any kind. It was mostly food and tapestry. She would have to look for a sword another time. There was someone she needed to see, which was more urgent.

She searched the area. How would she find Walis in here?

"Thief!" a man called, his angered voice in stark contrast with the otherwise cheerful sounds.

"I'm sorry." It was a child's voice this time.

Sin motioned toward them and her sight set on a girl no older than six. Countless bright blue braids fell to her shoulder blades. Her clothes were rags, covered in dust and dirt.

"Rat!" the man shouted and grabbed the girl's arm. The booth next to him was covered in freshly baked bread and other treats.

The girl clutched a small end piece of bread in her free hand. "My baby brother is hungry," she cried. "I meant no harm."

"Everyone pays."

Sin moved closer, her heart pounding as badly as her thigh. She didn't like the man's manners. He was cloaked in gold, a large sapphire ring glittering on one of his fingers, which was latched around the girl's wrist. Sin scowled, crouching, her hand finding the pommel of the dagger she had taken from the Boulder.

The baker lifted the girl up by her braids and flung her to the ground. The girl yelped but the baker didn't seem to care.

"Mongrels need to be put down," he snarled and lifted his arm.

"Hey!" Sin caught his forearm as it came swinging.

His narrow eyes met hers. "Don't interfere. I will have justice."

"You're six times her size. I think she's already paid the price."

"She's not paid at all," he growled, spit forming at the edge of his mouth. "These street rats think they can help themselves wherever they like because my wares are out. I'll not have it no more."

Sin pushed the dagger underneath his armpit, close enough for him to feel it sting but not enough to draw blood.

"I said, she's paid. Leave her be."

"None of your business. Get, or I'll call the guards."

Sin shook her head and dug out a few coins from her satchel. It was enough to pay for a quarter of his wares, if not more. "I'll take two loaves of bread as well as the end piece already had."

He glared at the coins and back at Sin, then took them from her palm. "The next time I catch her or any of her little dirty rat-friends, I'll not be so kind." He grabbed two loaves and chucked them at the girl.

Sin backed up against the child, keeping the dagger at the ready. She offered the girl a hand behind her back and pulled her to her feet before she finally turned and scurried off with the girl's arm in her hold.

They hurried past the next three booths, then slipped between a couple more where they could no longer see the baker. And more importantly, he couldn't see them.

Sin tightened the bindings around her thigh. A line of red had seeped through. The veins in her leg had expanded at the exertion.

"Thank you." The girl held the loaves tight under one arm.

"You shouldn't steal," Sin said.

"My baby brother isn't even past his second summer. I didn't know what else to do."

Sin sighed. "I understand, but you've got to look after yourself. They could hang you. For an end piece, no less. It's not worth it."

The girl started crying. "I'll try to do better."

"I'm sure you're already trying your hardest. I'm Sinyara. What's your name?"

"Blue."

"Pretty name."

The girl wiped the snot from her nose on her sleeve and smiled. The song from a flute sounded somewhere nearby and the girl turned to sprint off.

"Wait!" Sin called and ran after her. She shifted her weight as much as she could away from her injured leg. It would heal a lot slower if she kept this up.

Blue weaved between the crowd and slipped past a multitude of booths with ease. It was easier when you were little. Sin pushed past a number of people, repeating her apologies over and over again. Where did the girl go? The sound of the flute grew louder as Sin moved closer. She caught a glimpse of the blue hair and sped up.

She found the girl sitting alongside a group of other children in a small space by the walls surrounding the square. A fair amount of adults stood behind them.

"Then the dragons were gone," a man said. Sin

recognized Walis's deep tone. He sat on a stool with his back against the wall, his walking stick in hand. "No one knows where they went," he continued.

The children stared at him like he was the most magnificent sight they had ever laid eyes on, and Sin sat next to Blue. She massaged her leg, thankful for the chance to rest.

"Why did you run?" Sin whispered.

"Sh! I don't want to miss another word." She glanced at Sin and smiled, offering her a piece of loaf. "I figured you could keep up."

The baker might have been a brute, but he sure knew how to bake. The bread was airy, with a hint of nutmeg and just the right amount of salt. Sin only took one small bite, however, as the girl and her family clearly needed it more than her.

The story kept going for a while and Sin found herself immersed in Walis's words as much as the children did. There was something about him. But this was not the time to let her guard down. He was a Magical and a possible threat to Aradria. Perhaps his story contained clues? She didn't quite know what that would be, though she rather enjoyed hearing about how the dragons suddenly disappeared from Aradria, and how they were foreseen to someday reappear. In the end, Sin had to accept that it was nothing but a story.

The children clapped with intense enthusiasm and Sin slapped her hands together, too.

"That is all this old man has to offer for today,"

Walis concluded. "If anyone can spare a coin or two, that would go a long way to fill my belly."

A few people came up to him and left coins in his open hands before the spectators dispersed. Only Blue and Sin were left. The girl took Sin's hand and brought her to Walis.

"Hi," she said.

"Hello, Blue." Walis smiled and sniffed the air. "Ah, and hello to you too, Sinyara."

Sin grimaced. "How did you know I was here?"

"You smell."

Blue giggled. "Sinyara saved my life."

Walis tilted his chin up. "Did she really? That would be the second time that I know of when you have shown bravery and placed a stranger over yourself. My debt keeps growing."

"It was nothing." Sin kicked her foot between two cobbles.

"It was everything." Walis staggered to his feet. "Walk with me, my dear. And Blue, why don't you run off to your brother? I smell bread."

A blotch of red painted the girl's brown top.

"Wait. You're hurt," Sin said.

"I am?" Blue angled her body in an awkward position, tracing her fingers over her shoulder blade. "Ouch."

"Let me see." Sin gently pulled the girl's top up on her back until she saw the gash. It must have happened when the baker threw her to the ground. Bloody fool of a man. "This could get infected. You need to get it looked at immediately."

The girl tugged at Walis's sleeve and the old man sighed, lifting her to his lap.

"Is anyone watching?" asked Walis.

No one was facing them. Walis was in the shade now, too, and with the crowd occupied by the booths, they were easy to miss.

"Not that I can tell," Sin said.

"Good."

Walis placed his hand on the girl's back, and the magic surrounding him intensified. What was he doing? Was he about to perform magic? In broad daylight? Sin clutched her dagger, ready to attack. Her breath quickened and she stepped forward. She wouldn't let him hurt her.

The girl laughed and Sin lowered her shoulders. Blue jumped off Walis's lap as the sense of magic doused.

"Thank you." Blue gave Walis a quick hug, then squeezed her small arms around Sin before she hurried away from them into a nearby street. Sin shook herself and fell in step with Walis.

"What did you do?"

"I healed her. That is my gift." He took her arm. "You have a good heart, Sinyara, though I suspect the wounds in it travel deep. I'm afraid I cannot heal a wounded heart. That limp you've got, however, that could be fixed."

Sin raised her eyebrows. She was many things but no one had ever said she had a good heart. Her heart was full of darkness. Perhaps he would see that too if he had sight. He was right about a couple of things, however. Her heart was nothing if not an open wound, and she was injured.

"It's not that bad. It will be like it never happened in a few days." Sin decided to change the topic. Using magic like this, to heal, wasn't something she was inclined to do. "Eamon is well. He slept past the rising sun and my friends have taken him with them to Madame Rona. We found her establishment early this morning."

"You took my son to stay in a house full of meretrixes?"

Sin shrugged. "They had nice rooms and cost less than most places we saw. As long as we're not paying for additional services, that is. The women were quite friendly to Eamon."

Walis chuckled. "One is never too young to learn about the more shaded parts of life—or the brighter ones."

"Besides, he's not staying in Valano, is he?"

"No. He's not. I've made arrangements for him but I need to ask one more favor of you. I need you to take him to where he's going. I have eyes on me at all times, so I can't do it myself or I would."

"You said something about someplace safe. For Magicals? Though your son doesn't seem all that magical."

Walis chuckled again. He stopped, leaning both hands on his walking stick.

"Before I send you, though, there is something I need to do. Please don't misunderstand my request. I have no desire to make you my bedmate. I do have to ask if I can touch your skin, however."

"My skin?"

"Your shoulder, to be exact."

Sin held her breath. He knew about the brandings. If he touched her shoulder and found the mark, there was no way he would allow her access to what she needed. The alley they had entered was nearly empty. There was hardly a person in sight. What was she going to do?

Walis angled his head at her. "I understand your skepticism and I respect your right not to allow me to touch you. But I am trusting you with a secret that isn't mine alone, not to mention I'm trusting you with my son. I already know you won't harm him. Not now, at least."

He was waiting for her move. But she couldn't. Could she? There were no favorable alternatives. Her only chance was to try the truth, at least in parts. She angled her shoulder at Walis.

"Go on." She lifted away the part of her cape shielding her shoulders.

Walis reached out and found her forearm. He traced his fingers over the gauntlet and continued up her bare shoulder. There was no mark on that shoulder. Perhaps he would be satisfied with that? That was too much to hope for, though. He finished his inspection then gestured for her to turn. He repeated the process and his fingers glided over the mark of the dragon. Walis's brows lifted and fell until he allowed his hand to drop back on the pommel of his walking stick.

Sin braced herself. She wasn't sure what she could say to explain what he had found.

Walis tapped the pommel, tilting his head curiously. "I thought for sure I would find something." He shrugged. "Guess I was wrong. You're just another Magical who found herself at the wrong place at the right time. Here." He handed her a piece of parchment, closing her hand around it. "This will show you where to go and what to say. I thank you!"

Sin watched as Walis strolled further up the alley until he was gone from sight. How was that even possible? She grabbed her own shoulder, the one with the mark. It was smooth to the touch, no trace of her mark at all. A frown formed on her face as she stomped back to her new accommodation.

The door slammed into the wall as Sin entered. She quickly surveyed the room. Lacy, Rip, and Ward were the only ones there. Elaborate pillows and strands of fabric littered the space. The smell was rather uninviting, too, though Sin could not quite put her finger on what it reminded her of.

"Lacy," Sin said, her voice harsh.

Lacy turned from the mirror she was looking at and put a hairbrush down on the dresser. "That's one way to say hello."

"Did you do something?" Sin pointed at her shoulder, glaring at the Illusionist on her team.

"I did. Before we entered the city. I figured it was best to cloak ourselves. I wasn't sure I could do it."

"Mine is gone, too." Ward patted his shoulder, while Rip discovered the same thing.

Sin stomped her feet. "Walis almost had me figured out. He wanted to see if I had the mark of the dragon on me."

The room stilled for a moment and Lacy began brushing her hair again. "Well, what are you so mad about then? Seems to me I saved your butt."

"It would've been nice to know what you did. I could've outed us."

"But you didn't. I'm not sure how long the illusion will hold, though. I've never maintained one this long before."

Sin slumped onto one of the beds, sinking into the soft mattress. "I'm not sure it has to. The man is blind."

"Really?" Lacy tossed her hair back. "By the king, I'm good!"

There was no denying it. What Lacy had done was brilliant, and it had given them an alibi. Walis trusted them now. It didn't sit well with Sin for some reason, however. She didn't enjoy lying. Although it wasn't really a lie, as Walis had made his own conclusions and Sin hadn't known about the illusion Lacy had made.

"Where's Eamon and Mercy?" Sin asked.

Ward sat on the opposite bed, sewing a tear in his cape. The shades of purple on his cheek had acquired a more greenish hue. "Eamon wasn't feeling well, so

Mercy took him to Madame Rona for some tea and herbs."

The boy was sick? They should move him someplace where he would get better care as soon as they could. They couldn't spend time tending to a sick child. Sin unwrinkled the parchment still clutched in her hand. It was a map. At the bottom was a line of words.

"Do you know what this means, Ward?"

He came to sit by her side, glancing at the parchment. "I'm not sure. A password maybe?"

Mercy and Eamon entered the open doorway and closed it behind them. Eamon did look a bit the worse for wear. Dark circles framed his eyes that hadn't been there before.

"Hey, Mercy," Sin called. "Do you know what this means?"

"Hand it over," Mercy said.

Sin gave her the parchment and leaned over Mercy while she read aloud. "Skjulta Magica ith Lady of White. Visande Dej." Mercy scratched her nose. "I think it's an uncloaking spell. And the Lady of White part should make it fairly obvious."

"The House of Worship?"

"By the looks of this map, yes."

Sin exhaled heavily and fell back on the bed. She should have known something was wrong when they passed the Lady of White before. The terror she had felt was real, and it wasn't remnants of old magic she had sensed. It was actual magic, right then and there. It had to be where the opposition was holed up. How had she not seen it?

"Don't be so hard on yourself," Ward said and gave her a pat on the back. She winced as he hit her bruise but did her best not to show it. "None of us knew. And the place is cloaked."

Rip dumped down on the other side. "But now we know and we can take them down. Silly old fool, that Walis."

"He's not a fool," Sin retorted.

"I only meant... wait, why do you care what I call him?"

Sin shook her head. She wasn't quite sure what it was about Walis that made her react this way. The man was a Magical, undoubtedly a threat. But he had healed Blue with the touch of his hand. He had done something Sin thought she would never see, a magical act of kindness. There were no healers like that on Mount Fyra.

"I only meant that he appears intelligent. We still need to tread with care. Sorry I snapped."

Rip rolled onto his stomach, his body leaning into Sin and his face close to hers. "That's all right. I get it." He took her hand and Sin didn't pull back.

Ward glanced at them and his eyes fell before he rose from the bed to find his own.

"Practice in the morning?" he asked Sin.

She nodded. "First thing." She didn't have time to figure out what he was thinking as Nefero soared into the room, descending on Lacy's dresser.

"Falcon," Lacy exclaimed.

"Nefero," Sin cooed, sitting. The falcon flew over to perch on her good thigh. "Happy to see you. I guess it's time I sent my first report."

There were things she wouldn't tell Matteo about. She did have news, however, and she would tell him they had gotten a lead and might find the opposition soon. And she would ask him about Vilyur, ask if his horn had started growing and if they would wait for her return, so she could be the one to saw it down. He was her unicorn, after all.

"Ink?"

Mercy picked up a bottle from the dresser where Lacy sat and lobbed it to Sin, who caught it with one hand. She found a feather and a parchment and began writing. In a couple of days, she would hopefully be able to share news about the whereabouts of the opposition, too. She would not fail, and Matteo would be proud of her.

CHAPTER NINE

"I don't think we should go all at once," Sin said. "I'll take Rip. They're bound to be suspicious of us, even if Walis did send us, so it's probably better if the rest of you stay behind. There might be whispers to be heard in the city still." She glanced at Eamon, who had been put on bed rest until their departure. There were limits to how much she could say with him around. "I urge you to keep practicing your skills while we're gone."

Eamon sat. "I'm not going without Mercy."

"But—"

"No!"

Mercy batted her eyes at Sin and sat by Eamon's side, taking his hand in hers. "He does need some looking after. I'm really the best choice for that."

Sin blew out her cheeks. "Well, all right then. Mercy can come, too. But Lacy and Ward, you're staying—for now. I'll send word for you when I can."

"You're leaving me? With him?" Lacy glared at Ward.

"Perhaps you can use this time to find some common ground?" Sin suggested. It wasn't favorable to leave Ward alone with Lacy, but she had to believe that they were a team and that Ward could take care of himself.

"Don't worry." Ward propped himself up on the windowsill. "Her tricks don't work on me. Remember?"

"Be nice. Both of you." Sin turned and began packing. "We leave as soon as it's dark, so you guys better pack what you need as well."

It was still a while until sunset, so after they had packed and geared up, all they could do was wait.

Sin looked at her team.

Mercy fed Eamon some soup. The Venomizer was much kinder than Sin had imagined. Lacy and Ward studied a map of the city together and Rip... Rip smiled broadly at her while he whetted his knife. Perhaps they could do it, complete their mission, with the help of one another. It was a much stronger team than Sin had first envisioned. And even if she didn't trust all of them, at least not entirely, she didn't question their resolution or devotion to the cause.

"Going to get some air," Sin announced before she climbed out the window and onto the roof. The entire city was at her feet. Gold, silver, and copper veins glimmered in the twilight.

"May I sit with you?" Ward climbed to her side.

"Sure."

They sat for a while without talking before Ward turned to her. "Don't you think the city looks kind of magical?"

"I think it looks more like Lacy. Shimmering on the outside, dark on the inside."

Ward laughed. At least his laughs were better than his snores. "Perhaps, but it's beautiful. I can't imagine any Unspelled creating this without at least some sort of magical assistance."

Sin gave him a sideways glance. What was he trying to say?

His arms went around his legs and he rested his chin on his knees. "Do you ever wonder... I mean, have you ever thought that magic might be good?"

Sin fought the sudden instinct to slap him. "Why?"

"Even Unspelled are both good and bad. There are Magicals with abilities to restore and heal."

"Like Walis."

"Well, aren't those good things?"

Sin dangled her feet over the edge of the rooftop. "If I were to wound an attacker who went for my life, and Walis healed the attacker to try again, is that good?"

"But that's about choice. Don't you believe we can choose whom we want to be?"

Choose? What choice did they have? They were born in darkness, it was a part of them. There was no choice. "I'm not a good person, and neither are you. Magic corrupts all. Did your time on Mount Fyra teach you nothing?"

"I was only in the House of Air for a short while.

After I left my family, the masters kept me in a tower away from the others. I had to learn control or I would upset the abilities of the other fledglings. I spent a lot of my time reading and missing my family."

"You remember them?" Sin said.

"I was young, but yes, I remember their faces, my mother's lullabies, and my sister's laughter. I remember my father teaching me to whittle. And I remember a day when the Silverlings came to claim me."

"I don't remember anything like that. I only remember scaring my parents, and then Matteo came. I remember how he made me feel—like I was wanted."

They watched as the darkness swallowed the light and the stars twinkled in the night.

"We need to leave now. Can I count on you?" Sin asked. His words concerned her. Could she trust him if he didn't trust in the Order?

"I'm on your team, Sin. I believe in you, and I believe that we need to keep Aradria protected and safe. Threats to the Unspelled can't be tolerated. So, yes, of course, you can trust me."

Sin wasn't sure and it made her glad to know she had decided he was to stay in the city with Lace. His thoughts were borderline treasonous, though she didn't think he meant any harm. Perhaps he just wasn't as bright as Matteo had thought.

They climbed back inside and said their goodbyes.

Mercy helped Eamon dress.

"He has a slight fever," she said. "We need to take it easy with him." She tousled his hair and pulled a furry hood over his head. She made sure he was covered up in plenty of furs so he wouldn't get cold on the plains.

"Are you all right to travel?" Sin asked.

"All good," Eamon said. "Mercy is exaggerating."

He gave Mercy a big hug. In the absence of his actual mother, it was probably good for him to have someone mother him, and Mercy was doing a fine job of filling that role.

"Ready?" Rip asked, already standing in the open doorway.

"Ready!" Sin grabbed her haversack. "I'll send for you soon," she called over her shoulder as they left Ward and Lacy behind.

They went to fetch three of their unicorns and guided them through the empty streets of Valano to the gates. Sin pulled her cloak on tight and covered her mouth and nose with a scarf. The night gave her goosebumps.

GETTING OUT OF THE CITY WAS A LOT EASIER THAN GETTING in. No papers were required and no questions were asked. The unicorns trotted beside them as they slipped out of the gates and stepped onto the drawbridge.

Two large figures turned toward them on the other side.

Sin squinted. The moonlight illuminated the silver skin on the two Silverlings. They reminded her of younger versions of Matteo, broad shoulders and proud frames. They towered a head taller than Rip, stopping an arm's length in front of them.

"Evening," said the larger of the two. All Silverlings had scarifications on their heads and bodies. This one, however, had covered his entire forehead with angled patterns stretching all the way over his temples to the bridge of his nose.

"Good evening," Sin replied.

The smaller of the two frowned with hairless brows. "The boy. Bring him forward."

"The boy? What could you possibly want from an Unspelled child?"

The surge of magic in the air intensified as Mercy pushed ahead of Eamon. It was good that she wanted to protect him, though far too telling that something was amiss.

The scarred Silverling crossed his arms. "The boy. Now!"

They had to get off the bridge. The gates were closed at their backs, however, and the only way off was ahead. The water running underneath them was hardly suitable for swimming. Not that Sin knew how to swim, but that would be the least of their concerns if they tumbled into the moat. She had been a fool. Walis had warned her about the Silverlings, yet she hadn't paid much attention to it, she realized. Matteo was one of them, and so were all the masters at Mount Fyra. They were more her kin than anyone, even if they did not share the same reflection. Right now, though, these Silverlings were a problem.

The smoothness of the pommel of her sword brushed against her palm before the roughness of the hilt met her skin, and she folded her hand around it. She saw no other way if they did not allow them to pass.

"We only want to pass," she said.

"That's Walis's boy. Where are you taking him?" the smaller Silverling snarled.

Rip came to Sin's side. He glanced at her and put on his best smile. "We're only taking him to see an aunt in the village."

The Silverlings raised their shoulders as though they were a single entity. Their hands went for their swords and Sin gave Rip a nod. This was a deathmatch she might not be able to win. She recalled her training with Matteo and how she often lost. The Silverlings had spent their lives as soldiers, much like her and Rip. They were bigger, stronger; but not faster.

Mercy backed up with Eamon and the unicorns as everyone else drew their swords at once.

The ringing of steel on steel pierced the night. Sin cussed the throbbing pain in her thigh as she nearly buckled under the weight of the impact. She angled sideways and kicked the Silverling above his heel. He cried out and thrust his sword at her. The tip flew by her throat, only a hair away from cutting skin. The blade continued in a circle and slashed Rip's arm instead, causing him to drop his sword. His attacker took the opportunity to shove him to his knees before Rip punched him between his legs.

Sin kicked the sword out of her opponent's hand. It plummeted into the moat as she rolled sideways. His fist slammed into the bridge. When he raised his sword-arm again, Sin flung herself toward him and plunged her blade into his eye. He staggered back and tripped over the edge. The sound of a splash was followed by burbling water. Sin gazed into the moat. Increasingly large bubbles formed on the surface before a sharp fin appeared, glimmering in the streaks of moonlight. Growls and splashes of water issued from below as the Venatorfish dug into the body. The clear water turned crimson as the large creature gobbled up its meal and disappeared underneath the bridge.

Sin spun back. Rip!

The clanging of swords sang as she parried the remaining Silverling's attack while Rip scrambled backward against his sword. He grabbed it and threw himself at the Silverling again. Two against one. Sin lashed out but was forced back. They kept swinging at the Silverling. He ducked and parried, pushing them further and further toward Mercy and Eamon, who had huddled as close to the gatehouse as they could. It was like everything they did was defending themselves. She had to change tactics.

She screamed, as loud and shrill as possible. The Silverling winced and, in a moment of weakness, he exposed himself.

She handed Rip her sword and pushed him into their opponent's arms. The Silverling staggered. Rip extended his arms and thrust both swords underneath the Silverling's ribs on either side. Pulling the blades back out, Rip retreated. He crossed his arms and sliced the blades outward through the air to sever his opponent's head from his body.

Sin and Rip were left heaving for breath. She leaned her hands on her knees, staring at their victim. It was the first time either of them had killed a Silverling. It was necessary but tragic that they had forced their hands.

"Well done, Rip," said Sin.

"You too."

The sound of hoofs against the planks of the drawbridge grew closer.

"We have to go," Mercy said. "The watchmen in the towers. They've called for archers."

"Shit!" Sin shifted her gaze to the battlements. People were stirring behind the merlons. The shape of arrows was made visible through the crenels in the light of the torches that were lit.

"Let's ride!"

They flung themselves onto the unicorns. Sin kicked her heels and the group galloped forward as a rain of arrows battered the bridge and splashed into the moat behind them.

They didn't slow down until they reached the other side of the village. Sin rode next to Mercy, who had Eamon in front of her while Rip had their flank.

They followed the road back the same way they had arrived, eventually passing the remains of the barn they had burnt to a crisp. There was nothing but a pile of ash and charred pieces of wood left. Sin took a moment to look for any signs of the bodies they had left behind, but there were no traces to tell they had ever been there.

The sense of magic grew as they rode onto the plains and over the first sand dune. But Sin was prepared this time. There were no remnants of old spirits or forgotten magic on the grounds; it was living, breathing Magicals that created the intense concentration of magic. Those she could deal with.

CHAPTER TEN

THE SPEARS OF THE WHITE LADY APPEARED OVER THE horizon long before the entire building was revealed. Eamon coughed and the dark circles around his eyes were heavy, but his mood was weirdly chipper considering what he had witnessed on the bridge.

Sin stared at him. What was it about this boy that made people risk their lives to catch him? An Unspelled child shouldn't cause this much trouble. What was she missing?

"Wait here," she said to Mercy and Eamon while she and Rip ascended the wide crescent steps that led to the entrance of the House of the White Lady. An iron gate shielded the wide wooden door beyond, shaped and bent into a variety of depictions of Aradrian creatures: unicorns, elves, griffins, mermians and one large squirrel. The hinges creaked as Rip opened the gate. He grabbed a thick, crescent-shaped door handle and banged it decisively. The dull sound echoed from within.

Nothing happened.

"Try pulling it?" Sin asked.

Rip pulled until he had his feet on the walls and his forehead turned red. The door didn't budge.

"Try the spell?" Rip said.

"Right." Sin rummaged through her haversack until her fingers found the parchment. She unwrinkled it, narrowing her eyes. "I never was much of a spellcaster."

"You can do this." Rip leaned his back on the door, catching his breath.

"All right. Let's see ... Skjulta Magica ith Lady of White ... Visande Dej."

Eamon giggled.

The wind turned, tugging at Sin's hair. The sand whipped up behind them, building into a sandstorm. Dust and bones spiraled into the air. Not again! Sin shook her head, about to try kicking the door in. She stopped, however. It was as though the stars shone brighter than before. Something glinted within the particles of sand. She squinted. A square shape materialized on the sand dune a good distance away, surrounded by a white shimmer.

"There!" She hopped over the steps and onto the ground. "Come on."

The four of them got back on their unicorns and charged right into the heart of the sandstorm. They came to a halt in front of what now looked like a door, the storm still raging around them. Should Sin knock or try to open it? What if the door disappeared again?

Eamon pushed in front of her and knocked on the door.

The sound of a whistle issued from the other side and the boy smiled, then whistled a few short notes back before the door swung open.

"Did you know it was here the whole time?" Sin narrowed her eyes at him.

"Yeah. But it was fun to watch Rip trying to open the doors to the White Lady. It's been stuck for as long as I have memory."

Mercy bumped Eamon's shoulder. "I agree. That was fun."

Sin surveyed the area around them before they all trotted over the threshold. She turned forward to a blanket of white sand that disappeared underneath the lapping water from the ocean. The surface glimmered with golden shafts from the scorching sun. The ocean? Where were they? She looked back. The door was gone, and nothing in this place looked anything like any place in Caradrea.

"Merry meet," a woman's soft voice sang as Sin faced forward again.

"Merry meet," she replied.

The woman appeared between the line of trees with white stems and vines full of red roses twisting around them.

"I am Roziana. And you are?" She fastened a flute to her belt.

"Walis sent us," Sin replied as Eamon rushed forward and threw his arms around Roziana's waist.

"Roz," he cried. "I've missed you."

"And I you, little one. I'm absolutely thrilled to see you. I thought you were lost."

"They saved me."

Roziana glanced at Sin, Mercy, and Rip, no doubt inspecting their wounds, and the blood clinging to their garments and skin. "And now they have brought you here. Don't worry, child. You're safe now. Come. I'll take you to the others. You may leave your magical companions. They're safe here, too."

They left the unicorns on the beach and watched them gallop across the white sand. They seemed happy, Sin thought. They deserved it.

The group followed Roziana into the tree line.

"I'm Sinyara. That's Rupert and Mercy."

"By the Mother, I thank you. Sinyara and Rupert. And Mercy. Eamon is very dear to me."

"If you don't mind. Where exactly is here?"

Roz smiled. "This is our sanctuary. We are the Children of Rhonja, and we're under Siren protection at one of the Mar-Ôen islands. You just stepped into a portal."

They were on the other side of Aradria. The Mar-Ôen islands were Ûndan territory, the Land of Water— Lacy's birth land. This was about as far from home as they could get. And what had Roz said? The Children of Rhonja? They had named the opposition after the late Elemental High Monarch, a beacon of magic—of terror and destruction. It only solidified everything Sin thought the opposition stood for.

Roz led them onward on a path until they reached a large clearing. A variety of huts and perhaps a few hundred people occupied the area. Further on was an immense dry-stone building, with several levels of square constructions. A wide mountain with green growth rose behind it.

Roz caught her looking. "That's a temple. Much like the Lady of White, though this one was made for Njord, the king of the ocean. The Sirens have allowed us refuge. Any Magical in need of protection can come here."

Sin felt it. The concentration of magic was almost as strong as on Mount Fyra, though somehow strangely different. They had found the opposition—the Children of Rhonja—though this was nothing like Sin had imagined.

"There's a couple of free huts for you right here. There should be a barrel of water for you to wash at the back as well." Her gaze shifted up and down Sin. "Eamon already has a place where he usually stays with his father. I do hope Walis will return soon."

"He was afraid he was being watched," Sin said.

"He probably was then."

"I know he was. We had to fight off two Silverlings to get here."

"I'm glad you made it safely. Not everyone does. Have a look around and come find me later. I'll be in the infirmary inside the temple. We have many wounded today."

Roz left and Rip brought Sin to the back of the hut. Like Roz had said, they found a barrel full of fresh water, including soap and cloth. They took turns scrubbing each other's faces and arms.

"How are you feeling?" he asked.

"Fine. More than fine actually."

He tilted his head at her, his dark lashes framing his eyes.

"We had to take them out. There was no other choice if we were going to find this place."

Sin flung the cloth at the wall of the hut. "I said I'm fine, did I not?"

"You seem completely at ease," he snickered.

Sin sighed and sat on the grass. "I know we had to kill them but I wish we could have avoided it. They were Silverlings, like Matteo and our other masters. They must have had a good reason for wanting to take Eamon, though I have no idea what that would be."

Rip sat next to her and brushed away a short lock of hair from her face. "I get it. You and I, we did what we had to. For our Order, our mission, and for the Unspelled. Darkness conceals but somewhere in this darkness is hope."

Sin leaned her head on his shoulder, inhaling the scent of leather.

"What hope?"

"The hope that even though we are damned, we can certainly protect the Unspelled from animals like us. We have the chance to be great, despite what we are. Magic will eventually consume us, and the Order will make sure we can never hurt anyone again. In the meantime, we can do everything humanly possible to protect those who cannot protect themselves."

The words he spoke mirrored what Sin had told herself all her life. The day would come when the magic inside would suffocate whatever good there was in her. She only feared that it was already happening.

"We are Protectors and we will protect the Unspelled for as long as we can," she replied. "By any means necessary. The Silverlings died to serve that purpose, and it was not in vain."

"Can I kiss you again now?" Rip grinned.

Sin grimaced and stood. "No."

Eamon and Mercy walked around the corner of the hut. The boy was pulling at her sleeve, his blue eyes wide with expectation.

"Come on," Mercy said. "Eamon has something to show you. Don't get too excited, though, it's only a game."

Eamon dragged Mercy with him. Sin and Rip followed between the row of huts toward the temple. They turned around the corner at the foot of the ancient building where a bunch of children sat in pairs around a row of stone tables, playing cards. The group walked past and Sin instantly recognized the drawings on the decks.

"What's that game they're playing?" she asked Eamon, as if she didn't know.

"It's the Domi Enchantress." Eamon kept going. They found a place away from the others where they could play undisturbed. The stone table was all the way at the back of the temple, surrounded by thick under-growth and tall trees. Two decks of cards lay on the table.

"It looks complicated," Sin said.

"I can teach you. My father and I play all the time."

"I'd like that." It was the first time the boy had smiled at her. Sin had played this game with Matteo a hundred times over, but she enjoyed the look on Eamon's face. It felt good that he didn't seem so scared of her anymore. He seemed happy, but his pale skin and the dark circles under his eyes worried her.

"So." Eamon sat cross-legged by the table with a deck of cards in his hands, and Sin found a seat oppo-site while Mercy and Rip sat on the stones at the foot of the temple.

"This is all about strategy." Eamon shuffled his deck and gave a cough. He was still sick, though not enough to let it stop him, and Sin was happy to indulge. "You'll start with a deck, too. The cards are all different. If you look at the bottom here, you can see the power symbols, and on top, it shows which element those powers belong to, as well as which type of card you've got."

The card Eamon showed Sin was one she knew well. It had a drawing of a Seeker on it with the number ten. It was one of the better cards because of the rarity of Seekers such as Sin, and there were hundreds of cards in existence.

"And this is a land card." Eamon held up a card depicting Bermunnos Mountain. He continued to explain the different types and how the game was played, and Sin pretended it was all new information to her. It did take some time to master the Domi Enchantress, and Sin would still lose to Matteo more often than she won. It required a lot of tactical skill and focus, which was why she enjoyed it so much.

Rip watched them as they played, commenting every now and then where comments should not be made. It had Sin laughing, though. Such a simple thing as playing cards could really take the edge off from all the worries she had been feeling.

She met Eamon's eyes and his smile faded, his lips quavering. He put his cards down, pointing at Sin.

"What... what's that?"

Sin followed the line of his finger to her shoulder. The mark of the dragon was slowly becoming visible. She quickly pulled her cloak over it but it was too late. Eamon stood abruptly, cards flying off the table, his head turning wildly in every direction.

"Not a word, child," Rip said quietly, clasping the pommel of his sword in a manner that could only be interpreted as threatening.

A tear swam from Eamon's eye. "You're them. But you saved me from them, and now... I don't understand."

"You can't tell." Sin stood, her shadow falling over Eamon. What were they going to do? He would expose them and everything would be lost. Sin could not allow it, though neither could she bring herself to silence the boy. Could she?

"Say the word." Rip glanced at Sin and she shook her head, turning her gaze on Mercy.

"Can you do something?"

"Perhaps it's time we took him out?" Mercy pushed Rip aside, keeping one hand underneath Eamon's jaw while she ran her fingers through his red tresses. The boy's eyes widened in terror.

"I thought you liked him?" Sin put a palm on her forehead.

"He's sweet, but our mission comes first. Besides, Eamon here has a secret."

The boy squirmed in Mercy's hold.

"At your command..." Rip said, pulling his sword halfway out of its sheath.

It made sense. The boy knew who they were now. But if they killed him, how would they explain it?

"It's too risky. Mercy, please. Can't you help?"

The Venomizer pulled Eamon's head back by his hair, tightening her grip. His mouth opened in a silent scream and she spit into it.

"That's sick," Rip said, pinching the bridge of his nose.

"I told you not to kill him!" Sin stood, anger boiling inside. What had they done? "We are not to harm Unspelled!"

"Relax." Mercy let go of Eamon and smirked. "Someone really ought to pull that sword out of your arse. He's not an Unspelled, and I didn't kill him. I messed with his memory a little, is all."

"Wait. Back up."

"Sweet young Eamon here is a Shield. Like Ward. He told me himself."

Sin massaged her temples. Yet again she had been fooled by a Shield, thinking he was something he was not. But if that was true, what were they supposed to do now?

"And you didn't think that was information you should have shared?"

Mercy shrugged. "In due time."

"I'm confused. If he's a Shield, your magic won't work on him."

"I found a loophole," said Mercy and stretched on her toes.

"What loophole?" Rip came to Sin's side, his hand resting on the small of her back.

"Ward said his magic came from his heart, right? So, I simply poisoned Eamon's heart and made it weak—the non-magical way, with natural herbs and remedies. Then I caged it with magic. And now I've poisoned his mind."

Sin gaped. She had it all backward. For some time, she had believed Lacy to be the more callous member of her team, the most volatile. But Lacy was but a child compared to Mercy, and this was another level of cruelty entirely. She had been reading the Venomizer wrong, and reading Magicals was supposed to be what Sin did best. Lacy was malicious, and Sin had allowed herself to fall blind to her childish tricks when Mercy was the one she should have been cautious about. If anyone was corrupted beyond redemption, Mercy was.

Eamon blinked as he slowly came to his senses. "What happened?"

"You poor thing. You passed out." Mercy covered her shoulders and swaddled Eamon in her arms. "We'll get you to Roz."

Rip and Sin carried the boy between them while Mercy held his hand. Sin studied Mercy's face; the lines of worry around her mouth and the sadness coating her eyes looked real, even though it surely wasn't. Sin knew that now, and she would not forget how well Mercy could act.

They carried the boy up the steps to the temple and turned a corner. They found Roz in the infirmary in conversation with two other Magicals. Roz hurried over as soon as she laid eyes on Eamon.

"What happened to him?" Her hand went to his forehead. "Poor child! You're burning up. Come, we'll find you a bed ."

"You can go back outside." Sin gave Mercy a stern look. She didn't want her to cause any more harm. She lowered her voice. "Take a look around."

Mercy shrugged and let go of Eamon's hand. "Feel better soon," she said before she walked away.

Rip and Sin carefully laid Eamon down on one of the beds in the vast infirmary.

The room was full of people. Most of them had gaping flesh wounds, and the strong scents of iron and poppy seed infused the air. Their injuries were too familiar for Sin not to recognize what they were. These were battle wounds, from swords and arrows, and if she was not mistaken, some had been inflicted by magic. She could still see the vibrant shades inside the wounds, the remnants of the magic that had hurt them. But she could also see the magic they held on their own. Most of the wounded were Magicals themselves.

"What happened to all these people?" Sin asked Roz while the woman wetted Eamon's forehead.

Roz sighed. "Another failed attempt at a rescue. We're not supposed to attack yet but some are getting restless. And I don't blame them, there's a lot at stake. Still, we don't have a strategy—or the numbers—to take on our enemy yet. Or that's the general consensus at least."

"Your enemy? And who is that?"

Roz took a deep breath, putting the back of her hand on Eamon's forehead. "His fever is rising. I'm not sure what more to do. It's a risk but we'll need to get his father here as quickly as possible."

"I'll fetch him," Rip said.

Sin nodded. "Sounds good. Be quick, will you?"

"As the rising tide." Rip winked. "I'll be back before you've had time to miss me."

Roz grabbed his forearm. "Wait. No one can follow you or see Walis leave Valano. Stay in the shadows! Take this." She handed him a bracelet and gave another one to Sin. It shone with shades of amber and gold, smooth apart from a rising line of ruby stones across the middle. "This allows you to always see the portal to the island. Just say the words 'Visande Dej,' and the door will open."

"Great." Rip clasped the bracelet on his wrist, blew a kiss at Sin, and dashed off.

Roz finished tending to Eamon, then moved on to help others. "There's not much more I can do for him. Let's pray to the Mother that Walis will be able to heal him when he arrives."

Sin sucked on her teeth. She had thought Mercy to be caring for the boy when all the while she had been spoon feeding him poison. How had Sin not seen that? There was a lot she had not picked up on but she intended to keep her eyes wide open going forward.

There were several other women and men who helped attend to the wounded, and Sin eventually fell in step to help out. What else was there to do? Besides, she had some experience with wounds and it made the time fly by faster. And if she was lucky, she might be able to acquire more information about the attack Roz had been talking about, and what the plan was.

They worked through the night, and Sin finally found her accommodated bed at the crack of dawn.

Her mind was racing, trying to make sense of everything. They were on an island, transported to the other end of Aradria. They had found the opposition, though Sin was still in the dark as to what their objective was or who was the leader. Perhaps it was Roz? It seemed like it might be her. But Sin had to know for sure. And what was she going to do about Mercy... or Eamon, for that matter? Eamon was a Shield. Was that why the rogue team of Protectors had been after him? But why would they take him like that? Surely, no blood should have been spilled. The thoughts kept spinning in her mind until she could no longer bear it and left the hut to find something better to do with her time.

CHAPTER ELEVEN

SIN SAT ON THE SAND DUNE NEAR THE WHITE LADY, watching the falling sun and clutching a vial in her hand. Once they learned all they needed and the leader was revealed, she would slip the poison Mercy had made into his or her drink. It would look like a failure of the heart, nothing more. Sin hoped they would find out who the leader was soon. Keeping up pretenses was draining. The wounded in the infirmary made her especially on edge. There wasn't a doubt in her mind that those wounds meant they had also wounded others. Unspelled were at risk, and Sin had helped tend to the Magicals. She didn't want to stay on the island any longer than they had to. And despite her recent experiences out on the plains, she found more comfort on the desolate plains than on the healthy, vibrant island.

She put the vial into a pouch in her belt and retrieved a parchment, ink and a feather from her haversack. It was time to write another report. She would tell Matteo that they had infiltrated the opposition who called themselves Children of Rhonja, that she had learned they wanted to attack soon, though she did not yet know where or how, but she would let him know exactly how many of them there were. She wished she could tell him she had found the leader, too, but this would do for now.

She whistled as she rolled the parchment in on itself and bound it with a ribbon. It took a while before the familiar squawk of a falcon issued from above. Nefero descended to perch on her shoulder and Sin offered him a handful of seeds. The falcon happily helped himself to the seeds before he leaned his head into the crook of her neck. Sin enjoyed his company. Neither of them had to pretend they were anything other than themselves.

"Good boy," she said. "I can always count on you. How is Vilyur?"

Nefero clapped his beak and rustled his feathers, which Sin took to mean that her unicorn was doing good. She tied the parchment to Nefero's femur then sat for a while and stroked his feathers.

A couple of shadows stretched over the edge of the dunes in front of her.

"Fly now. I'll see you soon. Go!"

Nefero shot into the air and spiraled off away from the light and back to Mount Fyra.

Rip and Walis rode over the dunes a moment later; Ward and Lacy had come too. They galloped forward until they reached Sin's side.

"Where is he?" Walis asked as he climbed off his horse.

"In the infirmary still. He's the same as yesterday, I'm afraid."

"Take me to him. Please!"

Sin nodded to the others in greeting. She lifted her forearm and whispered the words that made the portal reveal itself before everyone stepped inside.

WALIS KNELT NEXT TO HIS BOY. HIS ALMOST WHITE EYES were bloodshot with concern.

"I'm so sorry I wasn't here," he mumbled. "But I am now." He lifted his head. "I need some space."

Rip folded his arms gently around Sin and backed up a few steps. The rhythm of his breath calmed her. Lacy and Ward sat on one of the few free beds next to them. They kept an arm's length between them, but at least they were not bickering.

Walis placed his hands on Eamon's chest and a glow like the sun itself encased the boy. What would happen if Walis healed him? Eamon would tell Walis everything, and they would have failed their mission. They might have to fight their way back to Caradrea, as well. She was ashamed of herself for thinking as she did. She wanted Eamon to be with his father. She didn't really wish for the boy to be sick or die, and yet she hoped he would not heal any time soon.

"What is this?" Walis whispered.

"What's wrong?" Sin asked.

"There's some kind of cage around his heart, like someone imprisoned it, isolated it from the rest of him. And I also sense some kind of infection in his mind. This is not any normal sickness. This was a targeted attack."

Roz moved away from one of the other injured and crouched down opposite Walis. "An attack? Can you heal him?"

"I can heal the sickness in his heart but the rest is magic. It will take more time."

"Was it them?" Roz asked. "Did they do this when they tried to kidnap him?"

Walis exhaled heavily through his nose. "I don't know yet but we will find out."

He sat there for a while, his hands working meticulously over Eamon's chest. The boy writhed like he was in excruciating pain. He began shaking and Walis pulled back, the glow from his magic dimming.

"I removed most of the thorns I found encasing his heart, but there's much more work to do."

"I think you need to let him rest for a while," Roz said, placing her hands on his shoulders.

"You're quite right. His body can't take much more. I'll let him rest and continue in the morning."

"Then perhaps we can convene with the generals and discuss other matters now?"

Walis nodded. "We'll talk later," he said to Sin before he walked off with Roz.

"Mercy really did a number on him, didn't she?" Rip squeezed Sin tighter.

She wriggled out of his arms and faced him. "I need to find out what they're discussing. Can you guys all find Mercy and see what else you might discover? Be discreet! Will you make sure they manage, Ward?"

"We'll be spiders in the dark," Ward said.

Rip waited until Ward and Lacy had left before he took Sin's hands. "Be careful, yes?"

"Hey. It's like Ward said. Spiders in the dark. Besides, I know how to handle myself."

"You sure do."

Rip stepped closer, moving his arms to his back, forcing Sin to step closer still, her arms wrapped around him.

"I might do something foolish and die," he whispered.

"You might."

His eyes locked on hers and his breath coated her lips before his lips found hers. A slight tingle began at her toes and spread through her body as the kiss deepened. Sin let go of his hands and pushed him away. There wasn't time for this.

"Go!" she said.

"I can die now." He grinned.

"Don't die. Just go."

"Kiss you later." Rip winked, then scurried off after the others.

Sin wiped her mouth with the back of her hand. She shouldn't allow herself to be distracted like that. Who knew what she might have missed? She hurried off after where Walis had gone with Roz and eased down a narrow hallway. She snuck forward through the gloomily lit passageway until she heard them.

Low voices issued from behind a woollen curtain, which shielded the people inside—and outside—from view.

"It's time." Roz's voice was low and yet determined. "We can't wait much longer. The children are growing up, and they have recruited too many of them."

"My girl," a male voice cried. "They took Marabella."

"I'm sorry." Walis's voice was full of compassion, and even sorrow, Sin thought. "I know what it's like to lose your child to that place."

"I know you do," the male voice said. "It doesn't make it any better, though. You and I both know what will happen to my Marabella."

"Walis. Please! Won't you give the order?" Roz pleaded. "We might not have the numbers but we're ready."

"My dear Roziana. I'm not sure we are, and I don't want to risk the lives of the entire Magical community to find out. I need to know we stand a chance at defeating Mount Fyra for good."

Sin gripped the wall with one hand, her breath quickening. They were attacking Mount Fyra! And Walis had the final say? She had discovered the true leader of the Children of Rhonja. She reached into the pouch hanging from her belt and retrieved the vial Mercy had given her.

"They won't stop, Walis." The man was almost screaming at this point. "You do know that? They will continue to kidnap whomever they think is a good match for their cause, and kill those they believe are too big a threat to keep breathing."

Kidnap? What were they talking about?

"I know all of that. I still believe we need a better plan of attack. I will not risk any lives if I don't have to. Haven't we lost too many to the Heartless King and his mercenaries as it is?"

Sin leaned on the wall heaving for breath, and a pebble fell loose. It hit the ground with a clank before she had a chance to stop it.

"Who's there?" Walis called.

She might as well reveal herself.

"So sorry if I'm interrupting," Sin said as she stepped into the room. She struggled to keep her voice even. "I couldn't help but overhear."

"That's fine, Sinyara." Walis sighed. "Roziana and Arcus. You can leave me now. I need to talk to Sinyara."

Arcus snorted. "This conversation isn't done."

"Later. I promise."

The two Magicals left the room. Their magic was undeniable, and the force of their powers was undeniably strong.

"Who are you, really?" Sin asked Walis when the others had gone.

"I am Walis Craven. I'm a Magical with healing

powers, and I'm the chosen leader of the Children of Rhonja."

That was all the confirmation Sin needed. Walis turned his back on her, fanning his walking stick to guide him toward a bench at the other end of the room.

Sin quickly grabbed two cups from a shelf, filling them with wine before she poured the contents of the vial into one of them.

Walis gestured for Sin to sit. "What can I do for you?"

"You could have a drink with me."

He gave her a half-hearted smile and accepted the cup she handed to him.

"You heard everything, yes? So what do you think?" Walis slowly turned the stem of the cup between his fingers.

"I think you're fooling yourself if you think you can just charge Mount Fyra and take over. Sounds quite mad in fact. You do have the numbers but I have seen the Magicals here. Most of them look untrained. Many of them are too young or too old to fight off anyone, specially trained combatants. Your people will die if you do this."

Walis chuckled. "We are all quite mad. But that's how you get when your children are taken from you."

"How so?"

"I don't know where you came from, Sinyara, though you have been a blessing so far. Not everyone is privy to how the Heartless King operates. He's madder than any of us. Power hungry and perhaps more full of grief than any one of us can comprehend. The loss of the High Queen turned the half-elf into someone cruel, someone... heartless." Walis lifted the cup to his lips.

The High King? The king was Sin's top commander, her guiding star. He was the Protector above all Protectors. What Walis said painted an entirely different picture.

"You said they kidnap children?"

Walis folded both hands around the cup, lowering it to his lap. He had yet to taste the contents. "Yes." He looked at Sin as though he could see her. "Now. I think it's time you told me who you really are. Because you're certainly no gem trader."

Sin hesitated but she knew all she needed to know now. They were alone and if the potion didn't kill him, she would.

"I'm an Aradrian Protector!"

Walis raised his eyebrows but didn't pull away from her. "You know what we call your kind here?"

Sin shook her head. "No." It had never occurred to her that the Protectors might be known by other names among the Magical community.

"Assassins," Walis said.

Her heart sank in her chest. Assassins. Was that what she was? She was a Protector, a beacon, a savior. But she was also a sinner, a Magical, and above all, a killer. It was what she had been trained for her entire life—to kill. How else could she redeem herself? Assassins were people who killed a target for coin, with no care as to whom they killed. That wasn't what she was.

Walis took her hand and Sin froze. Her instincts told her to pull her arm back, though something else made her listen to her heart instead.

"You're confused?" he asked.

Sin nodded, though he couldn't see her. "I'm a Protector. What you're saying makes no sense to me."

"Of course it doesn't. And I don't blame you for not knowing the truth about your Order. You did not create the monstrosities of Mount Fyra. The Heartless King and his Silverlings did that."

"He is your king, too. You should not speak about him in a voice like that. Mount Fyra is my home and you're telling lies." Sin stood, blood rushing through her veins as her breath quickened.

"When someone decides to kidnap children and turn them into their personal mercenaries, I could not care less what their title is. The Heartless King has not earned my respect. He was not a natural successor to the throne, sorcerer or not, he was not an Elemental. Mount Fyra is not the place you believe it to be."

"What do you mean, sorcerer? The king is no such thing. And I wasn't kidnapped!" Sin tensed and her hand found the pommel of her sword.

"Of course you were. One way or the other. Your parents, like many others, would have been presented with the choice."

She wanted to take his head for all his lies. Yet she didn't. There was something about what he said that resonated with her. It clawed on her, as if his words tried to break into a hidden cell somewhere in her mind. There was a memory that she could not reach.

"W-what choice?"

"To watch their child being torn apart limb by limb in front of their eyes, or to give her up so she might live. Hoping she wasn't killed in combat. You can imagine what most parents choose. It is what I chose."

Sin fell to her knees. Her head throbbed and her body trembled. The weight of what Walis said was too heavy, and no matter how strong she thought she was, she was not strong enough for this.

"As I said." Walis knelt next to her, leaving his cup on the bench. "I don't blame you. I place blame on those responsible, and that is not you."

Tears welled up and Sin wiped her eyes. She didn't want to cry. And for what?

"You said something before. About losing a child..."

"Sabine, my firstborn."

Sabine? Terror gripped Sin's heart. She knew that name.

"What were her powers?"

Walis cupped a hand under her chin and lifted her head carefully to face him. "She was a Bird—she could fly." He smiled gently. "You can cry all you like, child. It isn't a pretty tale. But when you are done crying, you need to make a choice, and quickly."

She sensed no magic accompanying his words and was expecting him to somehow try to force his story into her heart with magic. Somehow, this made his words more compelling. She didn't want to believe him, but somewhere inside she knew he was telling the truth.

At least one side of it. She had known Sabine. The tears flowed freely now and she allowed herself to fully feel the pain. It was like she had been ripped apart on the inside, as if her heart and mind were but fragments of a puzzle piece she had yet to put together.

Walis held her the entire time. She sobbed on his shoulders, curling up like a baby in his arms. No one had ever held her like this as far as she could recall.

"Why don't I remember them?" she asked between sobs.

"Your parents? I don't know but I assume they've played tricks on you to fog your memories. I know someone who might be able to help you restore them, though, if you wish it."

"Perhaps later. Right now I need to tell you something. And then you can tell me again if you blame me or not."

Walis stiffened. He pulled back, leaning on his elbows. "Go on," he said.

"Sabine? Your daughter. I remember her."

It was like the air stilled for a moment. The vibrant shades of Walis's magic dimmed as he waited for her to continue.

Sin sucked in a breath. She didn't want to, but he deserved to know.

"She was fierce. One of the strongest opponents I've ever met. She was so quick, her magic so vivid. Like yours. I... she was even my friend, for a while." Sin hesitated. Sabine had been her friend before they were paired for a deathmatch. She was the last friend Sin had ever had on Mount Fyra before her team was put together. "She was my third mark," Sin confessed. "I killed her. I killed your daughter."

It was Walis's turn to cry and he sobbed without restraints, wailing at the rock ceiling. When he finally quieted, he leaned closer again.

"I am sorry about what happened to her—and to you. It could easily have been the other way around, and Sabine could have been the one sent here to kill me. She might have died by your hand, but not by your command. I don't blame you."

"You should. You should blame me."

Deep lines formed on his forehead. "Even if a part of me does, I should not. But if you wish to make amends, if only a little, then I have a proposition to make."

"And I have more to tell you. About Eamon."

They stood. Sin knocked Walis's cup over and it clanked to the ground. The floor sizzled as the contents spilled on the stone. She had made her choice.

CHAPTER TWELVE

"WHAT DID YOU FIND OUT?"

Rip sat on Sin's bed when she returned to her hut. An almost empty cup stood beside half a jug of wine. His lips were painted red. The dim light somehow exposed the crags and scars on his face. The stubble on his cheeks had grown and was beginning to provide more coverage, though not enough to hide the proof of battles fought on his skin.

"Not much. They want to attack somewhere, though I couldn't get a grasp on what their target is." She sat next to him. The truth was too much to share at this moment. "They did say that they didn't have the numbers and that it was too risky. So I don't think we need to worry yet."

She felt bad about lying to Rip but she was only serving half a lie. He would have to know and she would tell him, but not yet. She wanted the night for themselves. There was sure to be trouble once she revealed what she had learned. Rip was such a devoted Protector. His reaction was likely going to be one of disbelief. Turning your back on the truth you have lived for most of your life is not easily managed. She should know. It was only the revelation about Walis's daughter that had made her see the truth of his words. All she wanted at that moment, however, was to forget.

Rip pulled her closer. "Well, then. If we have time not to worry, perhaps we can slow down a little?"

"Slow..." Her words were lost as their lips connected again. His hands moved up her thighs and under her top, his fingers tracing her spine. The blood pumped in her veins. He was not her first anything besides being the only one she had kissed whom she actually cared for.

She found his belt and undid the buckle, pushing his trousers down with her foot, continuing to kick off both of their boots. Her head was spinning and she needed it to stop. If only for a little while. Rip could help her do that and he would. He tasted like blueberries, sweet with a bitter edge. His sunburned skin pressed against hers and she rolled him underneath her, gently biting his ear. He rolled them both back around and kissed the scars on her chest. His deep breaths shut out the other sounds of the night, their hearts beating in synchrony. She took her top off. The rough touch of his fingers trailed the marks on her shoulders before moving down her body. She counted the marks on his shoulders with her hands, then locked her fingers in his hair.

They stayed like that for the rest of the night and Sin forgot about her failed mission and the lies she had been told all her life. If only for a night. Once the first spears of light entered the hut again, Sin knew she couldn't delay it any longer. It was too much to bear on her own, and she had to make him understand. He had to understand. If he cared for her like she believed he did, he would listen.

"Get dressed," she said. "I need to tell you something."

He did as she said without question and took her hand as they walked outside. Few people were out but Ward sat beside a hut close by, whittling an arrow.

"Good." Sin gestured at Ward to follow. He should hear this too. She glanced at the hut where Mercy and Lace were staying. There was no sign of them, which was a relief. They shouldn't be involved. If only she got the boys on her side, they could deal with the girls when they had to. And if not, it would surely be Sin's last day drawing breath.

A young man was carrying a basket full of clothes with a bar of soap on top, ambling up the steps to the temple.

"Hey," Sin called. "Do you know where we might find Walis?"

"At this time of day? In bed, or more likely at the ocean side."

Sin didn't know where Walis's hut was, so she dragged the boys into the tree line and followed the path back to the ocean. The birds had only just begun humming, their chirps multiplying with every added strip of light in the sky.

Walis walked barefoot in the water as they stepped onto the beach, his trousers rolled up over his knees. The shimmer of his magic was like the glow from the sun. It had frightened Sin the first time she saw it. Now, however, it made her hopeful. This man could not die. She understood that now. She had a new mission: To keep him alive and help him return the lost children to their families.

"Walis!" Sin waved as he turned, rolling her eyes at herself. She kept acting like he had sight, though it often seemed like he saw more than most others.

"Sinyara." He strode out of the water, the sand sticking to his feet. "Who is with you? Wait... Blueberries and a strong scent of resin. Young Rupert and Ward, I presume."

"Yes," Sin said. "Just us, though."

"Have you come to kill me or did you decide to let me live?"

Killing him was the last thing Sin wanted to do. She had decided the moment she spilled his drink.

"I've brought the boys so they may learn the truth. As I did. I was hoping you could help me convince them."

Walis smiled broadly while Rip's hand slid around Sin's waist.

"What's going on?" Rip whispered.

"We have been played for fools, Rip. Mount Fyra isn't what we thought."

"What are you rambling on about? And why did Walis ask if we wanted to kill him?"

Ward spun his freshly made arrow in his hand. "I think he's their leader, and he knows who we are."

Walis chuckled. "You're much brighter than I believe your friends give you credit for, young Ward."

Rip unsheathed his sword, his other arm still around Sin's waist. "Say the word this time. You don't have to do this yourself."

She folded her hand around his, lowering his sword arm. It was no surprise to her that he would act this way but it stung all the same. He was devoted to their cause—like she had been less than a day ago. It would take a lot to convince him that the Order wasn't as they had been raised to believe.

"We're not doing it. Please. Allow him to explain and you'll see the truth, too."

Rip grimaced and dumped down to his bottom. He took off his boots and buried his toes into the white sand. "Enlighten me," he said with a hiss. Sin did not recognize him as the man who had just spent the night with her.

Ward embedded his arrow in the white sand next to Rip and sat beside him.

They stayed there, silent and listening for a long time, while Walis told them more or less the same things he had told Sin. All the while, she had her eyes on them, watching for misgivings or any chance they might attack either Walis, or even her. They didn't. Rip's face, however, was hard to interpret. He made all sorts of twitching of his nose and gestures with his eyes. His lips were tight as a string. No smiles or signs of sorrow, but a frown was slowly deepening.

"That is all," Walis said.

Rip stared at his feet, wiggling sand off his toes. "Sin is my commander. Where she goes, I follow. Though I'm not sure I believe a word of this. It sounds utterly ridiculous. Our king is supposedly a sorcerer, and a dangerous one at that? If that is true, he would surely be a target himself. Why would he want to create an army to kill those like him?"

"Fear." Walis tapped his walking stick with his index finger. "When he took the throne—and I mean took it—the Elemental rulers fell, and the magic of the world shifted into something Aradria did not recognize. Archenon fears that those powers will return and that his seat of power would crumble if it did. Eradicating his enemies and controlling the magical community goes a long way to prevent that from happening."

"Sounds like something you made up to keep Sin from slashing your throat."

"I think it sounds about accurate," Ward said. "I've long suspected something was wrong."

Rip pulled a face at Ward and stood. "I need to think."

Sin put her palm flat on his chest. "Look at me."

His gaze fell on hers, his dark lashes like a cloud shielding his amber eyes.

"Do you trust me?" she asked.

"I have never trusted anyone. All I have is my faith

in our cause. No matter if this is true or not, it doesn't change the fact that magic is treacherous. Our mission is still the same. Or mine is." He leaned closer, taking her hand. "I do trust you, however. But you have been fooled by a man trying to save his own life."

She took a deep breath. This wasn't going as smoothly as she had hoped. Still, it wasn't a surprise that he would act this way. "You can't tell the girls. All right?"

"You ask me of trust. What about him? How can you trust this man? How can you cast aside everything we believe in—us—for him?" He gestured at Walis.

"I just know it's true. You might not trust him but you know me, don't you?"

"I won't tell the girls."

Sin squeezed his hand. "I need to know you're still on my team, Rip."

He lifted his arm and kissed her palm before he let go of her. "Team Sinyara. What a joke." He spun on his heels to walk off, then lingered. The magic surrounding him increased in intensity, his body rigid.

Sin bit the inside of her cheek and curled her hands into fists. She looked from Walis to Ward, then back to Rip. He wasn't team Sinyara anymore. He probably never had been. He was a Protector, an assassin, through and through. And even though Sin no longer believed their cause was the right one, she was the same as him. An animal at heart, feral and unforgiving. She crouched, every muscle straining against her skin. Whatever came next, she would deal with it.

Rip's hand went for the knife in his belt. She couldn't let him throw it. He spun back around and Sin lunged at him as his hand pulled forth the knife. His arm arched over his head. She clasped her hand around his wrist while her feet kicked him to his back before she planted her knee on his chest to keep him down.

"Don't," she hissed.

"I'm doing this for you. For us. For our guiding star and king."

"No. Rip, please! If you do this, I will stop you."

His gaze softened for a moment. "Then you'll have to stop me. Because I'm throwing this knife, and when I do, I won't miss. Choose, Sinyara."

It was a choice she didn't want to make but he was right. And her choice had already been made. She gave him one last chance, however. She loosened her grip slightly and his arm pushed back up. It was settled the moment he went for the kill. Sin tightened her grip again, forcing his wrist down at his chest, sliding the knife into his heart.

Rip coughed. Blood rained from his mouth and seeped out of the wound in his chest. The life drained from his eyes as he whispered his last words.

"Traitor."

"No," Sin cried. "If you weren't so stubborn."

With a last effort, he spat in her face. His body slowly waned as his breathing slowed. His eyes rolled back and the magic surrounding him departed in bursts with his final gasps, drifting away into the air. Then it was over. Rip was dead—by her hand. And in his last moments, he had hated her.

Sin clambered off him and backed up in the sand, hugging herself. She rocked back and forth as tears spilled from her eyes. The white sand around Rip's body was increasingly darkened by blood.

Walis came to her side. "You saved my life, child. My debt keeps growing."

She looked at Ward through the veil of tears. He was crying, too.

"It was the only choice," Ward said. "I'm sorry it was yours to make."

Lacy and Mercy strolled out of the tree line. They took one look at the scene in front of them and Lacy gave a scream so loud the birds ascended from within the canopies, filling the air with the noise of their batting wings.

The girls ran to Rip, and Lacy put his head in her lap. "Who did this?"

Mercy pointed at Sin. Her bloodied hands revealed her. "She did."

The Illusionist scrambled to her feet, stepping over Rip's body. "I knew she couldn't be trusted."

Sin exchanged a look with Ward. She filled her lungs with air and they charged forward. He had been practicing. This was not the same boy she had fought in the arena at Mount Fyra. He shielded his body this time and never left himself exposed. As Mercy's toxins would not affect him, Sin went for Lacy.

The girl was quick on her feet, though not as quick

as Sin. The Illusionist backed up, then plunged a knife into Sin's leg as she was about to trip her over. Sin cussed at the pain. A knife in her leg was not about to slow her down, however. Lacy's fingers worked as fast as she could between blows. It wouldn't be enough. Sin swung her blade, cutting across Lacy's forearm, then the other. If Sin could avoid it, there would be no more killing this day. She rolled on the ground and kicked Mercy at the back of her knees. The Venomizer tumbled into Lacy and both girls fell forward. Ward and Sin were on top of them an instant later, their fists meeting the girls' faces simultaneously until they both blacked out.

MERCY OPENED HER EYES FIRST AND LACY WASN'T FAR behind. Both girls were tied up, hands and feet bound to separate trees.

"What now?" Ward asked.

Sin shook her head. "I don't want to kill them."

"I have a suggestion," Walis said, leaning on his walking stick. "There is a dungeon underneath the temple. It's sometimes used to interrogate assas— Protectors. We can keep them there for as long as necessary or until, by some chance, we're able to convince them of the truth."

"I don't think they would help even if they did believe us. But it does sound like our best option for now," Sin said.

Ward walked over to Mercy and tied a scarf over her mouth. "We don't want her spitting on anyone," he said.

"Spitting?" Walis asked.

"She's a Venomizer."

"I see. Which is why you spilled my drink yesterday, Sinyara?"

"Yes."

"I'm glad you did, though I'm sorry to see you lose friends today."

"These two were never really my friends," Sin said, knowing it was true.

Though Rip had been one. More than a friend even. And she had killed him. It would haunt her for the rest of her life what she had done to him. She felt sure of it. And yet, he had given her no alternative. She cussed him for the fool he had been while her heart mourned for the friend she had known.

"She didn't lose everyone," Ward said, taking her arm.

She leaned into him. Ward had been right all along. There was both good and bad in all people. Magicals and Unspelled alike. And he had been by her side the whole time. How had she not seen it before now?

"I am glad to have you, Ward. Though our team seems to have shrunk somewhat."

Walis drew a line in the sand with his stick and stepped over it.

"Your team is one of hundreds, my dear. The line has been drawn, and now I need your help to do what this community has wanted to do for decades. Bring our children home, and never be afraid to lose them to Mount Fyra and the king ever again."

How could Sin have been so blind? Her thoughts went to Matteo. He had been her mentor, her friend. All in all, he had been a father to her when she had no other. At the same time, he was the one who had robbed her of a father in the first place. She shook herself. But he had always treated her with kindness, had he not? It would take some time for her to fit all the pieces of the puzzle together. She had found her path, however. And she would not stray from it.

No matter the cost.

CHAPTER THIRTEEN

THE DOORS TO THE DUNGEON SLAMMED SHUT. THEY HAD not been able to convince either Lacy or Mercy to swap sides. The girls would have to stay on the island until Sin found a way to silence them without spilling blood or until the time came when Mount Fyra was no more than a desolate mountain.

Sin nodded at the two men who had been assigned the task of guarding the girls. They had also been the ones tending to Rip's body as Sin could not bear to do it herself. Hershel and Garreth were twins, both of them Magicals. They tapped their swords and nodded back as Sin and Ward climbed the steps to the outside.

Ward fiddled with a bowstring in his hands. "What do we do now?"

"We go to meet Walis and the others."

They passed the row of tables where the decks of the Domi Enchantress lay at the ready for anyone who wanted to play. No one was playing, however.

"Sin," Ward started.

"Yes."

"I'm frightened."

"Why wouldn't you be? But you need to quench that fear, for fear is a weakness."

He twined the bowstring around his fingers. "Rip would have killed him."

"I know."

"You had no other choice."

"I know."

"I just mean, you should not blame yourself so much."

"For the sake of the Mother, I know!"

Did she, though? Ward's words made sense. It was the same words Sin kept telling herself. But the guilt. The guilt was ever present, like a claw clutching around her heart, like talons scratching at it, shaving away one small piece after the other to the point where she wanted to rip it from her chest for all the pain it caused. Still, pain, like fear, was a weakness, and she could not allow herself to be weak.

"I didn't mean to snap at you," she said. "You're a great friend."

"You're wired. I get it."

They walked the steps to the temple and found Walis and the others in the room where Sin had first come to acknowledge the truth about her life.

"Good. You're here," Walis said.

Roz and Arcus stood beside Walis looking at a map that had been unfolded on a stone table. The younger of the three Magicals were heavily armed, even though there were no threats around. Not that they knew of.

"What is the meaning of this?" Arcus asked. His short tangerine-colored hair was a mess, like he had not washed it for at least a month. The brown leather garments he wore did not hide the strong body underneath, however. This was a man who had trained for combat.

"And why are they here?" Roz stepped in front of the map, shielding it with her body. Her wide sleeves did a good job of hiding what was beyond but Sin had already seen the map of Caradrea, and the red cross marking Mount Fyra.

"Ease down, Roz." Walis took her arm. "I have news. I'm giving the order."

An audible silence pervaded the room. Roz's eyes teared up, her hands folding over her heart. "You are?"

"About time," said Arcus.

"Yes. And Sinyara and Ward here will be our most important assets."

"They are children." Arcus frowned. "What do they possibly have to offer?"

Walis waved his hands for them to sit while Sin and Ward lingered by the doorway. "Now, keep your heads where they are when I tell you this. And let me finish before you voice your concerns. Sinyara and Ward are here to help. They know the secrets of Mount Fyra that we do not, and they alone can help us bring down the walls."

"And how is that?" Arcus asked.

"Arcus, I told you to wait."

The man contracted his lips into an almost square shape as Walis continued.

"Like I said, they will be our way in. And the reason why is because they are Protectors."

The two Magicals leaped to their feet. The field of magic grew around them in shades of copper and amber.

What were they?

"Stop!" Sin called. "Stop right there."

They froze and scowled at her, and she took a step closer.

"I am trained to kill. I'm a Seeker. I know your moves before you do yourselves. And Ward is a Shield, like Eamon. You won't be able to use your magic at his touch and I'll wrench the life out of you before you take a second breath. So don't. I'm not in the mood."

Roz and Arcus backed up, their magic retracting. They sat back on the bench, goggling at Sin.

"Well." Walis exhaled in quick breaths. "I think what Sinyara was trying to say is that they are on our side. They want to fight with us. Right, Sinyara?"

Sin tilted her chin in agreement, and Ward cleared his throat.

"I was isolated for a long time because of my power, my... gift. I no longer believe it a curse. It allows me to remember things the other fledglings and Protectors don't. If you mean only to take out the masters and not harm the children, then I'm with you."

The masters. Matteo. Had Sin thought this through?

"Is there another way? I mean, besides killing anyone?" she asked.

Walis looked at her with drooping eyes. "Perhaps Arcus could show you? Arcus?"

"If you'll allow me?" The hilt of a knife glinted in his belt as he crossed the light of the torches. Arcus showed Sin his palms as he carefully approached her. "I can show you events that have happened in the past. They are exact retellings. That is my gift."

Sin flinched. Powers that messed with the minds of people were the most dangerous of them all.

"I have never heard of that power before."

"I'm not surprised. They would not want you to see what I'm about to show you."

Sin angled away from him but Walis nodded. She had to trust him. If not, why had she done what she did to Rip? "All right. But don't try anything or Ward will stop you."

"Understood."

Arcus put his hands on her temples and her head was instantly flooded with images. There was no cohesive story at first, then it was as if one image got picked away from the others to plant a scene in her head. It was a farmhouse, near the ocean in another land. A banner of purple and gold blew in the wind from a sailboat. It was her birth land—the Land of Spirit.

A man and woman walked toward the farm, the man carrying a small girl in his hands. The girl had light lilac hair, like Sin. Her heart skipped a beat. It was her! The girl was her and the people were her parents.

They walked into the house while the girl played with her father's nose. Sin's father. Her father's hair was white but her mother had strands like her own. Someone knocked on the door and her mother took the girl, hiding her in a closet.

"Stay very still, child," she said and gave Sin a kiss on the forehead before darkness surrounded her.

The doors to the house opened with a creak and Sin watched through a crack in the wooden door of the closet. Matteo's face appeared in the doorway. It was the one memory she had from before. His silver-tinted skin, his purple lips, and his smile. But his smile looked different somehow. It wasn't gentle or warm like she remembered. It was menacing.

"We have come for the child," he said.

"We sent her away," Sin's father lied.

"Did you now? Then why did my falcon mark this as her whereabouts?" Nefero swooped in to perch on Matteo's shoulder. The falcon squawked and shot forward, tapping his beak on the closet doors.

"Good bird," Matteo said.

Sin wanted to scream. Her heart was ripped apart yet again.

"Please," her mother cried. "She's our only child. She has done no wrong."

"Maybe not yet, but her magic is dangerous and the king cannot allow those like her to roam freely. She is coming with us, or we can kill her now. I'll happily tear her to pieces right here. You decide."

Her father found Sin in the closet and took her in his

arms. He kissed her on the nose and stroked her long curls over her shoulders. His eyes were full of tears and Sin felt her own tears swimming freely down her cheeks.

"Remember us," he said.

"Why, Father?" Sin heard herself say. "Why would I forget?"

Her mother kissed her, too. She folded her arms around Sin like she never wanted to let go.

After a while, Matteo grew impatient. "The child," he bellowed.

"Let us say goodbye," her father cried. "Have you no heart, Silverling?"

"Now." Matteo snapped his fingers and two other Silverlings entered the house, wrenching Sin from her parents' hold.

"Mother, Father," Sin cried. "Don't let them take me. I don't want to go."

"Don't forget who you are, Sinyara," her father called after her as Matteo took her in his arms and carried her over the threshold.

The memory disappeared as Arcus lowered his hands, the images slowly replaced by the stone room in the temple.

Sin dropped down, swaying on the balls of her feet. "That's not how I remember it."

"But this was the truth of how it happened. The memory you had before was not real." Arcus went back to sit beside Roz.

Everything Sin knew was a lie. Matteo had betrayed

her from the very first moment and she had looked at him with awe. He had taught her so much, yet withheld the things she should have known. Sin shook and Ward sat beside her, allowing her to lean on him as the shivers in her body decreased.

"My parents. Where are they now?" Sin said in a whisper.

Arcus shook his head. "I don't know. Some of the parents have been killed over the years attempting to rescue their children, but I did not know yours and I did not recognize them in your memory. I'm sorry."

"You all had a child taken?" Ward asked.

They nodded.

"I'm from Caradrea. Perhaps you know mine?"

The others looked at each other and Arcus turned his palms up. "Maybe. What do you remember?"

Ward told them everything he knew but Sin stopped listening. Her head throbbed. Once this new mission was done, she had to find them. Dead or alive, she needed to know what had become of her parents. They hadn't given her up freely the way she had been told. She knew that now. They had given her up so she might stand a chance, however slim. And they had loved her, magic or no magic. They had not cared that she had powers. She was not the troubled child Matteo had always said she was.

The anger at Matteo's deceit boiled in her veins. She would help the Children of Rhonja, and they would eradicate every last one of the masters at Mount Fyra.

The king would not recruit children ever again if she had any say in it.

"Sin!" Ward crouched in front of her. "Did you hear? My parents are alive. Roz knows them."

"Are they here?"

"Not anymore, but Roz knows where I can find them."

Sin held back a sob. He had a family to get back to. "Then you should go."

The smell of wet soil entered Sin's nostrils as Ward embraced her. "I will. But not yet. First, we save our people."

"All right," Sin said. First, they would save the fledglings. Then they would find their parents, assuming any of them still lived to do so.

It was time to get strategic. Distant memories and dreams of a family could not be a distraction.

"Come," Walis said. "Let's talk."

"How is Eamon?" Sin asked in a low tone.

"Better." He smiled. "Let's talk business, hm?"

They gathered around the map. It was not flat like it had first appeared. It had elevations and dips to mark changes in the environment.

"It's only a few days from the portal to the foothills of the mountain," Ward said. "We can't go up the same way we came down, though. There are scouts all over the place, either side of the mountain. Still, the north ridge is harder to patrol."

Roz traced her fingers over the map. "I agree. It will take longer but the north side has more cover."

"What of the Vulkan eagles?" asked Arcus.

Sin shook her head. "They are not a threat. No one commands them, so they won't be a bother until after the fight if there are a lot of bodies still on the ground."

"The bigger issue is how to get inside," Walis muttered.

"I guess that's where we come in." The elevations on the map pressed against Sin's palms. "We can go, distract the masters, open the gates and let you in."

"They're bound to be suspicious with just the two of us," Ward said.

He was right. It would look strange. She would have to come up with some sort of plan to conceal their intent.

"I'm not sure what to tell them but I can send a report with Nefero ahead of time and let them know we're coming. Perhaps say we need to speak to them in person while the others are still working on stopping the Children of Rhonja. I could tell them I have completed my task."

"You mean killed me?" said Walis.

"That was your task?" Roz took a couple of pins out of her red hair, allowing it to fall to her waist. "And we let you into our fold like a friend."

Walis took her arm. "Good thing we did, Roz, or we would never have found a way in."

"I suppose. When do we leave then?" Roz narrowed her eyes at Sin, then looked at Walis.

"You're getting ahead of yourself. This needs planning. I would say we are going to need about a month's time before we can even think about heading out."

"A month? It will be winter by then." Arcus slammed his fist on the table and his eyes shifted to Sin. "What could have happened to my girl in another month?"

"How long ago was she taken?" Sin asked.

"It has been more than three months."

"And how old is she?"

He sniffled and wiped his eyes. "Four. My Marabella is only four."

"Then you shouldn't worry. The children are well treated. They will train her for at least a year before her first deathmatch. No one is sent into the arena without proper preparation. Especially the youngest fledglings who aren't old enough to have practiced their magic yet."

Arcus gave a sigh of relief. "Thank you. That gives me hope I haven't lost her yet."

"Glad to give you something other than concern."

Roz bit her lip and Sin already knew what she wanted to know.

"Tell me then. About your child."

Roz folded her hands. "My Hannah is nine, assuming she still lives. My Ulric is only seven." Her voice trembled. She sucked in a breath and closed her eyes briefly. "Hannah was taken three years ago, and they came for Ulric last summer. They both had the power to read minds."

Sin mulled it over. She didn't recognize their names,

though she hadn't encountered a lot of Mindreaders, and to her relief, she had never killed one.

"I'm not sure I know them."

"I do," Ward said. "Or at least one of them. I was only in the House of Air for a short time but I remember Ulric. He was really annoyed when he couldn't read my mind. I think he arrived shortly after I did."

"But you must have been taken years ago?" Arcus asked.

"I was kept in a tower... long story."

Roz wrapped her arms around Ward. "Thank you." She repeated the words several more times before she withdrew.

Walis cleared his throat. "Well then, shall we get back to planning?"

Sin was relieved to focus on something other than tears and pain. She welcomed the chance to plan their attack. They leaned over the map and talked for hours. Plans were put forth, and ideas were dismissed. It was a good thing they would still have a few weeks to trace up their plan because nothing they had thought of so far was going to get the job done.

Sin found her bed again at the crack of dawn. She rolled over and something dug into her back. Her hand folded around a hard, smooth surface. She pulled it out from underneath her and sat. Rip's whetstone. He had used it frequently to sharpen his blades. She folded her fingers around it and lay down, hugging the whetstone to her chest.

Then she wept.

CHAPTER FOURTEEN

SIN WATCHED NEFERO FLY OFF OVER THE CARADREAN plains with her latest report, narrowing her gaze. That bird was not what he had seemed either. She had believed him to be loyal. Everything, even him, had been a trick. He was never her friend; Matteo was his master as much as he had been hers. She lay back in the warm sand, the grains running over her palms and through her fingers. The plan they had ended up constructing was risky but anything else they had come up with was worse.

This report was the most important piece of the plan. Everything had been set in motion by this one message, and there would be no going back from here. They couldn't count on a surprise. The masters had to know she was coming back with Ward without the rest of the team. They had to be prepared, confident. She didn't feel like she was either of those but the plan was the best they had.

She had strayed only a little from the original report and asked about Vilyur, asked that she got to be the one to saw his horn. It was her unicorn; she had claimed him. It was only right. He would have grown so much. But that one request was not crucial to the plan one way or the other, only to her own desires. And no matter how she felt about the Order at this point, magic was still something to be feared.

Most of her report was genuine. She had revealed more than she would have liked, keeping her sins out of it. Walis had thought it best that true words about the Children of Rhonja and about him was the only way her retellings would appear believable. So, she had revealed Walis's name, the number of people on the island and even that there was a portal on the Caradrean plains. She had not mentioned their exact location, however. That was too much of a risk.

"Hey," Ward said as he walked to her side. "Ready?"

She squinted at the sun and jumped to her feet, drawing her sword—Ward's sword—from its sheath.

"I still feel bad fighting you with your own sword," she said.

"I was never that close to it, and besides, I got me a new one. You can always give it back another time."

Sin lunged forward.

Ward knelt, raising his blade to meet her blow.

"Good," she said as the sound of metal against metal sang in her ears. They had practiced every day, and Ward was a quick study. He had even begun building some muscles on his fair-skinned body. The days in the sun had given him a ton of extra freckles on his chest, too.

Ward kicked his foot out, sending Sin to her back. She rolled backward and rose in a crouch.

"Very good." She gestured with her free hand for him to come closer. He ran forward with his arms in the air. Sin ducked and drove the pommel into his stomach, then grabbed his foot and sent him tumbling forward, much like that first time they fought in the arena back at Fyra.

He fell face first into the sand.

She tittered. "You have to shield your body. Be patient. Funny I should have to tell that to someone who is a Shield."

She offered him a hand and pulled him to a sitting position before sitting next to him. "So, I've been thinking. How do you suppose your power works?"

"When I was younger, any Magical I came in contact with or even laid my eyes on was affected. They would always find their powers restored once they had put enough distance between us, though. Now I have more control and can choose whom to target. Apart from by touch, that is."

"Anyone you came in contact with, huh? How many would you say you can magically disarm at once?"

"I know that they kept me away from Fyra for a reason, though I'm not sure how wide of a web I can create. I guess the only way to know for sure is to practice."

Sin bit the inside of her cheek, her mind racing. There was something about his power she didn't quite understand. "Maybe it's like you're a magnet?"

"Never considered that. But yes. Sort of."

"But where does it go?"

Ward slid a hand over his head. "What do you mean?"

"The magic has to go somewhere. It stands to reason that it moves host. So when you stripped me of my power in the arena, they were never gone, they just weren't mine to inhabit anymore." Sin put her chin in her hand. "I think the only place it could go is to you. Like a magnet, you pull the magic inside you."

"I guess. Maybe."

The wind blew across the plains to reveal a number of bones sticking out from the sand. Sin stood. Her thoughts spilled through her mouth.

"And if shielding your heart with the breastplate makes your power useless, and the mixture you take inhibits them, like with Eamon and the herbs Mercy fed him, then that would make your heart the magnet. Of sorts."

"I've never really thought of it that way."

"Because they didn't want you to. The masters. They knew something we don't." She paced a circle in the sand before she stopped. It was ridiculous. Then again, perhaps not. Powers were known to grow over the years, to evolve and become stronger, while the person controlling it became more corrupted. If she was right, Shields would be the most powerful people in all of

Aradria. And the Children of Rhonja had two of them. "Ward. Do you think that you're able to channel the magic you take and use it yourself?"

"I... I've never tried."

"Try. Lose the breastplate and stop taking that mixture you take."

"I stopped using the breastplate as soon as we came to Valano. And I haven't taken a drop of the mixture since that day in Yirin's stables. I can thank Mercy for that." He grinned.

She laughed and gave him a pat on the back.

"Perfect. Now all we have to do is find someone to practice on."

He tilted his head at her. "Can't I try it with you?"

"How would you know if it worked? I would look like any Unspelled to you once you take my powers."

"I guess we need to find someone else to practice on." He turned his gaze north. The dark walls of Fyra stood like a pillar in the sand a few days' walk away from them and Sin frowned. She drew her blade through the sand and sheathed it. "No time to waste. Let's go and find out what you can do!"

A GENTLE BREEZE BRUSHED SIN'S FACE. THE ROOFS OF hundreds of huts spread out below. Standing at the top of the temple somehow reminded her of looking out at the world from an outpost at Mount Fyra. She had never seen the full picture of things from the mountain she named home but her view had changed. The people of the camp were a mix of Magicals and Unspelled. The Magicals, however, carried with them the signature of the power they bore within. A myriad of colors stretched out, slinking between the huts and the Unspelled of the camp. They were almost evenly matched with the amount of resistance they would face on Fyra. Numbers, however, was not what would win or lose this fight.

Ward angled his head upward. He stood at the top of the stairwell leading into the temple. His palms turned up and his eyes closed. The signatures of magic from the people on the stairs vanished in an instant. The effect spread like the wind blowing out a small flame. The colors faded one by one by the nearest huts before the signatures could no longer be extinguished.

Sin sighed. He had disarmed perhaps a hundred people. If he could teach Eamon to do the same, then that would mean they could possibly take away the powers of nearly two hundred of the Protectors and fledglings. It wouldn't be enough on its own. Still, it would make for an advantage.

A thundering crack bellowed from below. Ward stood among a pile of rubble at the bottom of the stairs. The stone steps were in ruin. He looked up at her and mouthed a few words. Though she couldn't hear him, she could just about make out the words on his lips. "The strength of a Boulder." Sin grinned, turned on her heels, and sprinted down the inside stairwell to meet Ward at the ground. He had actually managed to take a power and make it his own. This could be exactly what they needed.

A dark red shade slipped away from Ward to snake itself around the blacksmith standing by a nearby hut. He was staring at the hammer in his hand, swinging it up and down as if he was testing the weight of it. He shook his head and walked away with his power returned.

"I owe you an apology," Sin said while climbing over the rubble.

"Why?" Ward smiled at her, flexing his arms and smiling sheepishly.

"I underestimated the usefulness of your power—and of you."

"So did I." Ward crouched and lifted a rock into his hands. "We need to clear away the rubble and fix the stairs."

An increasing amount of people were gathering in front of them, the whispers multiplying to the extent that it overpowered every other noise.

"We could use the help of that blacksmith," Sin said while trying to lift one of the larger stones.

A young girl with yellow hair and black skin walked out of the crowd. Her round yellow-colored eyes stared from Ward to Sin and down at the stones. She nodded and started to pick up what she could from the ruins. More people followed. A man helped Sin remove the stones she could not remove herself, and the space was soon clear of rubble.

The yellow-haired girl smiled at Sin before she walked off and the crowd dispersed.

Ward and Sin sat on what had been the third step of the stairs, dangling their feet.

"We're leaving soon," he said.

"I know."

"Do you think it will work?"

"It has to." Sin took Ward's hand. "Or we die."

CHAPTER FIFTEEN

THE PEOPLE ON THE ISLAND HAD BEEN BUSY OVER THE LAST few weeks, preparing for their departure. The black-smiths had been working especially hard, and Sin had spent most of her time helping the Boulder-smith out in the forge, when she wasn't training with Ward or discussing strategy with Walis, that was. The feeling of hard labor was greatly satisfying and had taken her mind off Rip during the day. She still kept his whet-stone underneath her pillow, however. She had regained her strength and then some, and her wounds had healed nicely. Even if she acquired new ones during battle practice every day, they were superficial and didn't stop her from working hard.

She lifted her hammer and let it fall, repeatedly and with precision. The embers sparked and the steel bent. She folded the steel and repeated the process. It would be a while before it was done but she enjoyed watching the steel fold.

A shadow entered the forge as Ward appeared by the entrance.

He had been helping the bow makers and spent a lot of time with Eamon. The boy had quickly recovered after Mercy was locked away, and Ward was now practicing with him every day. Walis didn't want his son to come with them to Mount Fyra, and who could blame him.

Ward leaned on the arched stone entry to the forge, watching her. She plunged the freshly forged sword into a bucket of water. It sizzled and boiled before she drew it back out. Drops of perspiration trickled down her spine.

She had a silent hope that she could convince Matteo to make everyone lay down arms, so they might shut the Order down in a more peaceful manner. He would likely stake her to the walls before he agreed to something like that, though. Still, she had hope, something she had not had before.

"Walis says we leave tomorrow," Ward said.

"Great." Sin said with less enthusiasm than she had meant to.

"Are you ready for this?"

"Are you?"

They shook their heads at each other, both smiling. It wasn't going to be easy, and this might be the last smile they shared for some time, or at all.

"I just finished another lesson with Eamon. The boy is talented, I'll tell you that much." Ward twined his fingers, his gaze shifting from Sin to his hands.

"Walis doesn't want him to fight, though Eamon insists."

"I'll talk to Walis. The boy has to be there. Hopefully, he won't have to kill anyone."

Sin for one was glad to have Eamon do his part. She understood the old man's reservations about bringing his child to a deathmatch like Fyra had never seen, but he had to come; the plan depended on it. Walis knew that, too, and he would see reason. The power of the Shields would be their foremost crucial weapon in disabling the strongest of the Magicals on Fyra. And there were plenty of them. But even without their magic, they had fighting skills and experience that went beyond what most of the members of Rhonja had.

Ward's fingers traced the walls before he straightened and squared his shoulders.

"I was wondering if you would like to walk with me? It's our last night on the island and I would like us to remember it."

She wiped her brow, no doubt smearing it full of ash. "Why not?"

They left the forge and found their way to the beach. The ocean had long since washed away the traces of what Sin had done to Rip. But she still remembered the exact spot where he had lain before they had carried him off to be buried nearby. He was probably still turning in his grave because of his resting place. It was customary for Protectors to be burned, their ashes spread from the highest peak on Mount Fyra. Perhaps she would return to the island and dig him up to do him the honors once this was all over. If she lived that long.

"It's been more than a month now," Ward said. "And he's still on your mind?"

She grimaced. Where was Ward going with this? "Why wouldn't he be?"

"He was an animal, Sin."

"So am I."

"No. You, you are something else. And he was never anywhere close to worthy of your attention. Nor am I, I suppose."

He needed to stop. Sin clasped a hand around his forearm.

"Whatever you're about to say, I don't want to hear it." She glared at him, her mind willing him to stop talking.

"We can't always get what we want."

Like she didn't know that. Still, he could choose to stay his voice. He stared right back at her. Didn't waver.

"I have known for a while how I feel about you, and I accept that those feelings are not reciprocated. But I want you to know that I have hope that someday I might prove worthy and that you might look at me like you did him. I don't wish to distract you from our plans, and so you don't have to say anything right now. But if we survive this endeavor, which I have faith we will, then I hope you will allow me the chance to court you."

Court her? She burst out laughing.

Ward crossed his arms over his chest. "What's so funny? I'm pouring my heart out and you're laughing?"

"I'm sorry, Ward. It's just... did you ever think that courting me was the right move? I'm not someone you can win with trinkets or sweet words."

"Forget I said anything." He trudged onwards and Sin ran after him.

"I really am sorry. Ward. You're my friend. My best friend, I believe, and I don't want to complicate things by trying to make this into something it's not. I wish I could feel like you do but I don't." She inhaled deeply. "I do care for you."

He sighed, staring out over the lapping waves of the ocean. "All right then, we're friends. I'll accept that. For now."

They walked the beach for a while and talked about everything other than his feelings for her, which was how Sin liked it. Things had changed so much since they left Fyra. She had thought Ward to be weak, a liability even. He was none of that. In fact, he was the strongest person she had ever met.

When Sin returned to her hut, Walis was waiting for her. He sat on the end of her bed, gazing into nothing.

"Walis?"

"Good evening, Sinyara. I hope I'm not disturbing you. I won't stay long." He had his walking stick in one hand and held a sheath with a sword in the other.

"Of course not. I was just about to turn in. Big day tomorrow."

"It is. Which is why I wanted to give you some-thing." He presented her the sword.

"You're giving me a blade?"

"This was my wife's. My first wife, that is. She passed after a failed rescue attempt about ten years back. I held onto it in the hopes Sabine might one day return. Now that I know she can never wield it, I want it to be yours."

Was he mad? He wanted to give away the sword intended for his daughter to the person who took her life.

"I couldn't possibly accept."

"I want you to have it. Please."

Sin took the sheath and drew the sword, feeling the weight of the blade in her hand. It was a perfect fit.

"I am honored. Thank you." She stared at the sword in awe. The pommel was made of Fyranian black stone, the hilt bound with black leather. Two small rubies were inlaid on each side of the pommel to make eyes for what looked like the head of a dragon. Though simple in its design, the dragon was beautiful craftsmanship, and the guard had been made to look like wings. She did not deserve this.

"Are you still having doubts?" Walis asked.

"It's just... I don't deserve this gift. I'll take it because you want me to. But I don't believe I have earned it."

"You saved my life, Sinyara; you saved Eamon's life. You have earned this and more."

"Two rights don't absolve me for all the wrongs I've done. Or those I'm about to commit. I'm an animal—a killer. Always was. There's nothing but darkness in my heart."

Walis patted the bed next to him, inviting her to sit. She hesitated then dumped down by his side.

"Everyone has darkness in them," said Walis. "All people, magical or not, carry within them the chance for doing as much bad as they do good. It's not about what you have done or who you believe yourself to be. It's about the choices you make and why you make them."

"What do you know about the darkness?" Sin raised an eyebrow at him. He seemed to live his life in the light more than anyone she had ever met, though there was magic in him. She was curious to know how he could resist the pull of its corruption.

Walis angled away from her. "Did I tell you how I lost my sight?"

"You did not."

"It's not a tale I usually tell. Roz is the only one here who knows, and that's simply because she was there."

Sin stared at her new blade as Walis continued.

"It was around the time when word got out that the king had begun hunting Magicals. The first children had started to disappear. I was about your age, perhaps a bit younger. Roz and I worked in the salt mines off the east coast of Khâlâra. My father thought it best to hide me in the mines rather than risk that I got caught performing magic in the city. He thought the mines, however dangerous, would keep me safe. Roz's father had the same idea. But we were young, we didn't know or care about the repercussions. So we used our magic. I once healed Roz in front of a whole group of miners. I'm ashamed to say this, but I enjoyed the looks they gave me." He held his breath for a moment, cupping his hands around the pommel of his walking stick. "Our families were poor, and we decided that we could easily make one or two barrels of salt disappear."

"You stole?" Sin blurted.

"We did. And we did it again. And again. We thought we were invincible. Until we got caught, that is. Roz got a slightly different treatment than I did. The Silverling commander of the mines had heard about my powers to heal, so he didn't take my hands like one would most thieves. He wanted me to be able to heal him and his men whenever convenient. So he had his men tie me down and take turns shoving salt into my eyes."

"That's horrible."

"We were in the wrong. Though the commander was one of those who chose to act on his more sinister instincts. He kept Roz in his chambers and had me lashed at his pleasing. That is where I met Eamon's mother. She was a Shield, and the commander used her to stay Roz's power."

A Silverling had done this to him; taken his sight. The atrocities of their kind were becoming more and more evident. They were nothing like she once believed. It made her feel less bad about the Silverlings they killed in Valano.

"How did you escape?" she asked.

"That's just it. We became so full of hatred that we

devised a dreadful plan to get our revenge. We didn't just want to escape. One day, when the commander went to visit the mines, we made sure he never came back out. The casualties were many but we were free of him."

"You killed him, and the miners, too." It was hard to believe that Walis was capable of something like that. The red-haired Magical he called his friend, however. Sin could picture her doing it.

"We did. So, you see, I'm no better or worse than you are. But I feel guilt and shame every day. That is what separates us from someone who has surrendered completely to the darkness. They act without remorse."

"I've killed with no remorse."

"But why is that?"

That was a good question, and one Sin had not thought to ask herself. "I never knew differently, I guess. My orders were always clear and there was honor in death. Besides, it served a higher purpose. The fledglings who passed would have avoided living long enough to experience the horrors of what magic does to others—and to themselves. I never felt bad about killing them."

The truth of her words was horrific, now that she was given the chance to think about it. They were true, all the same, however. She really was a daughter of night. Even now.

"And how did you feel after Rip?" Walis asked.

Sin bit the inside of her cheek, an iron taste washing over her tongue. Killing Rip was the worst thing she had ever done. It had hurt her more than any wound she had acquired. Still did.

"I think about him every day and I sometimes wonder if I did the right thing."

Walis smiled gently. "And that is how I know there is more to you than darkness, Sinyara. All you need to do is trust that as well. Trust in yourself."

Was he right? Was what she felt about killing Rip tied to guilt, or was it more about her betrayal to him and to the Order? She wasn't sure. And if Walis had it in him to kill, then he was as bad as the rest of them. So was Roz. Did all their good deeds to help and heal others rectify the sins of their past? Had they changed when they wanted her to help them kill Silverlings and others like her—other Protectors? And who was to say that they would not once again succumb to the feral magic within?

"Are you taking Mount Fyra for revenge?" Sin asked.

"No, my dear. This is about rescuing those we can, and stopping the Order from taking any more children from their families. Magic isn't evil at its core. Good or evil is decided by the acts of those who wield it." Walis swung his walking stick carefully in front of him. "I'll see you in the morning, Sinyara."

"You can't see."

"Figure of speech." He chuckled and left the hut.

Good or evil. Was it as simple as making the choice? She wasn't a good person. Everything she had ever believed was based on Matteo's words: Magic corrupts all. Perhaps he had his reasons for taking her to Fyra, and perhaps she hadn't seen the whole picture when she glimpsed that moment from her past. Had she made a mistake killing Rip?

She shook herself. She had encountered both good and bad since she left Fyra. Atrocities committed by both Magicals and Unspelled. The baker in Valano whom Blue had run from wasn't magical, yet he wasn't good. The rogue Protectors were definitely bad. Walis healed people. No matter his past, he spent his days doing good now. And then there was Ward. She had yet to see him do anything to be considered evil. She had once told him he was a bad person, like her. That wasn't true—he was good. He was a Magical, and he was good.

Sin's fingers slid over the smooth leather of the sheath in her lap. She unbuckled the sheath she wore and placed it under her bed. It had not been the right sword for her, and she had held onto Ward's blade for too long. He had acquired a new one since then. A sword was like a friend, however, and it was time she gave it back. She placed her new blade under the bed next to Ward's before she eased under the covers, her hand slipping underneath the pillow and wrapping around Rip's whetstone. Tomorrow they would leave and, if she survived, she would come back to this place, to dig him up and take him home.

CHAPTER SIXTEEN

THE FROST BIT SIN'S CHEEKS. THE WHITE COVER OF WINTER had already fallen over the forest on the north side of the mountain. The ground was a sheet of white, and the tall trees and thick snow gave them good shelter from the scouts on Mount Fyra to the east.

Six hundred or so men and women were not easily concealed. Sin angled her head back. Hershel and Garreth rode with Roz in front of the next group of fifty people. It was a slow trot through the snow.

Sin glanced at Ward, who rode by her side, his shoulders squared, his chest jutting out. He finally looked like a warrior, and now he would have to act the part. Their job entailed going into Fyra on their own, and Ward might be forced to kill in cold blood. So far he had avoided it as best he could and she wished with all her heart that he never had to become what she was. Not just for his sake, but for hers. She needed to believe that magic was what Walis said it was. However much

Sin wanted to believe there was another side to magic—
a good side—she was yet to feel entirely convinced. To
take Mount Fyra, they would have to spill blood. Plenty
of it. Moreover, they would have to use magic to help
them. What would happen to Ward when he used his
power for this purpose? Granted, it would be for a good
cause, though was there such a thing that could absolve
them of their crimes? An excuse to kill those like them,
not to mention their Unspelled masters?

"What's on your mind, Sin?" Ward caught her gaze.

"I was just thinking it's time we made camp and did
our practice runs for the day."

"I promised Eamon we would try to expand his
power. Again."

It had not been easy to convince Walis to allow his
son to tag along for what promised to be a bloody fight,
but he had at last conceded as their plan depended on
Eamon and Ward's powers. He would not be fighting as
much anyway, not physically at least, and not without
taking powers from those around him. That had been
the deciding factor.

Sin inhaled the freshness of winter. "Everything
hinges on the two of you. He has to learn, and he has to
do it now. You have practiced with him for weeks."

"He's been close on several occasions. I believe he's
ready."

"He has to be."

Walis rose a fist in the air a few paces ahead of them,
signaling for the group to stop. Roz raised her fist in
turn. The signal was repeated every so often by the

assigned lieutenants in charge of their groups. They would camp here for the night, and Sin and Ward would begin their ascent in the morning. The army she had brought consisted of a variety of people, some skilled and trained combatants, though most of them were simple farmers and parents who only wanted to save their children, no matter the cost. Their motivation might be what saved them, though Sin feared it was more likely to be their bane.

She planted her feet firmly in the snow and, once they had settled, followed Eamon and Ward to a nearby clearing to practice. Walis and Roz came, too. The boys practiced their fighting skills first. Ward had improved so much that he could now teach Eamon—with Sin's guidance from the sidelines. They would need more help for the next part, however.

"Anyone with a bruise or some kind of wound?" Ward called.

Sin rolled her eyes. Which way did they want her to turn?

"I have a cut on my forearm," she said. "Feel free to try that."

Eamon took his father's hand and cupped his other over Sin's forearm. He closed his eyes, taking shallow breaths. The chatter of his teeth drummed in Sin's ears.

"Relax," Ward said. "Deep breaths. Focus on Walis's power, then find your intention. I know you feel it move."

Walis nodded at the boy. Sin saw a glimmer of magic

as it slinked away from Walis to latch onto Eamon before it was gone. She was powerless too.

They waited.

"It's not working." Eamon's eyes fell.

"Keep trying," Walis said.

"But how? I can feel your magic in my veins. I can even see ember-like colors surrounding Roz. But that is all."

Sin smiled. "That means you're using my power, Eamon. It is working!"

The boy raised his eyebrows, shaking his head. "It is? I still can't heal you."

"Perhaps because you can't use both our powers at once?" asked Sin.

"When I use mine," Walis said, "I try to imagine what it is I'm trying to heal, then I extract the pain into myself and release it. I think you need to clear your mind and decide firmly on your intent."

Eamon rolled his sleeves up, the hairs on his arms rising against the chills of winter. "All right. I'll try again."

The snow fell as heavy sleet. They would have to return to the camp soon. But they needed Eamon to learn. Fast. Sin licked the moisture from her lips and the cold crept up her arm. Then, a sliver of warmth entered her veins before the heat wrapped around her wrist, all the way to her elbow. It wasn't painful. It was comforting; soothing and calm. Then it was gone.

Eamon lifted his hand away and grinned.

"It worked. It bloody worked."

"Language," Walis said, though he was smiling, too.

Ward crouched next to the boy. "Well done, Eamon. Really well done. We might just prevail after all."

Roz stood, brushing snow off her trousers. "We'd best get back. There are still things to prepare before Sin and Ward leaves us." She folded one arm around Eamon, the other over Walis's shoulder. There was a bond there that had grown stronger over the last month. It had probably been there this whole time, Sin had simply failed to see it. The three of them looked like a family. At least, that was how Sin imagined a family to look like.

A sudden blow to the back of her head almost made her fall head first into the snow. Cold shivers ran down her neck and she turned, snarling.

Ward was already rolling another snowball in his hands.

"Don't even..." Sin turned quickly and the second snowball flew past her.

"Missed," she called. She grabbed a handful of snow, ran forward and threw herself at Ward. He fell to his back before she shoved the snowball in his face. Her vision blurred as he returned the favor. They rolled around in the snow until they were both on their backs, heaving for breath. Sin laughed and rolled to her side to catch Ward batting his arms and legs.

"What are you doing now?" She shook her head at him.

"I'm making a snow-lady."

"You look weird doing it."

"So? You look weird. Your hair is all stiff and wet at the same time."

Sin tilted her chin up, her eyes on the sky. The clouds abated above. The snow had stopped and the stars twinkled.

"We should go back. We'll freeze to icicles if we don't get out of these clothes and into something dry."

"That would be bad."

Ward gave Sin a hand and pulled her to her feet before they found their way back to the camp.

She shifted her attention back as a familiar squawk sounded somewhere over the treetops. That sound used to be comforting, she thought. It wasn't anymore. The falcon was a traitor as much as Matteo, or Sin herself. If that falcon could talk, they would all be dead come morning.

CHAPTER SEVENTEEN

THE WIND TORE AT SIN'S COAT AS THE GROUND disappeared beneath them. The white crowns of the trees spread far and wide, and Sin was relieved that she could not see their group underneath the covers.

A steep stairwell similar to the one on the east side of the mountain aided their ascent. This one was even more narrow than the other, however, and they were forced to climb behind one another. There would be few campsites this side too, and in a couple of days, they would have reached their destination.

The cool air promised another snowfall soon and she could only hope that the rest of their group caught up with them before the masters figured out what they were planning.

"You all right up there?" Ward called.

Sin angled back at him. "Nearly at the first campsite, I think. All good."

They didn't get a chance to speak much more than that. The whistling wind drowned out most other noises and made conversing difficult. It gave Sin time to think. The words she would say to Matteo had turned over in her head more times than she could count. He knew her better than she knew herself, which scared her more than she liked to admit. It was a fair chance that he would already know what she was up to. She hoped she had the element of surprise, however, as there were other things in play, which Matteo did not know about.

The ground leveled out as they reached a plateau on the mountainside, the first campsite.

Sin dumped her belongings close to the walls and collected the logs shielded by the mountain to start a fire. Her fingers trembled when she removed her gloves. Sores and cracks in her skin stung when faced with the cold. Fighting against the shivers in her body, she retrieved a piece of flint from her haversack and started trying to light the fire.

"Shoot!" she exclaimed when she dropped the stone between the logs. It nearly slipped out of her fingers again as she picked it back up.

"Here," Ward said, taking the flint from her hands. His own fingers were shaking too, but the fire soon licked the air.

"Maybe we should have waited until summer," Ward said through chattering teeth.

"We couldn't wait."

"I know. But it's freezing."

Sin could not deny that the cold was troublesome, though they had all agreed that they couldn't let the children stay in Mount Fyra when they had the means that might save them. The castle walls would provide more of a shelter, though the winters were always brutal on Fyra.

"You've become a decent warrior these past months." Sin gave him a smile.

"I had a good teacher." The sound of cracking ice rumbled down the mountainside and Ward shifted his gaze. "Did you notice the scouts earlier?"

"There were two in the tree line, another two about halfway up on the steps further south. And I'm pretty sure a couple are watching us right now."

Ward held a hand over his mouth so no one could read his lips, even though Sin was sure the scouts were too far away to read their faces at all. "I hope the illusion holds."

Sin nodded. They were well prepared but one misstep could cause the entire plan to fail.

"We have done all we can. If that isn't enough, then perhaps there is no saving the fledglings."

She took Ward's hand and placed her head in his lap. He folded his body over her, stroking her hair for a while.

"I wonder what they're like," Ward said.

"Who?"

"My family." He sighed heavily. "I remember them,

but it's been so long, all I have are fragments of memories. Do you think they forgot about me?"

"Not possible."

"You know I'll help you find yours, too, right? I
won't leave you alone until I know you have found
them."

Sin stared up at him. He had such a gentle heart,
and he had become the best friend she could have
asked for. She wished with all her heart that she could
love him as he deserved.

"You should stay with your family, Ward. I'll be fine
on my own. No need to waste precious time on me."

"Allow me to decide what is precious to my heart,
all right? I don't expect anything but I did agree to be
your friend, and this is what a friend does. So no more
arguing with me on this. It's decided."

They stayed in silence close to the flames. Both of
them knew what they were about to walk into and
neither of them looked forward to it. Instead of
addressing their concerns, they took turns to rest and
feed the fire, keeping it going through the night. As the
light of day flooded the ridge of the mountain, they
were already far past the campsite, heading for the next
one.

The wind was not as brutal as it had been the day
before, though the mountain was especially treacherous
this time of year, and the temperature was about to
drop as they climbed higher. The air would thin, and
they would already be worn by the time they could
enter the gates. It was bearable after having lived on

Fyra for years. It would be worse for those who were not as used to the substantial altitude. If their plan worked, however, they would be able to infiltrate the Order and gain the advantage they needed.

She could only hope the masters didn't see it coming.

CHAPTER EIGHTEEN

THE GATEHOUSE LOOMED IN FRONT OF THEM.

Sin grabbed Ward's arm. "Are you ready for this?"

"I have to be," said Ward.

She released her hold. She had to be as well. As soon as this was all over, she would help Ward find his parents. Then she would travel to Êvina to search for her own family. First, however, they had to face the masters.

A familiar face waved down at them. Everett, the Protector they had saved at Yirin's stables, stood guard. He whistled, and soon after the screech from the rising grate pierced her ears.

Sin lingered for a moment, sucked in a breath, then followed Ward into the lower bailey. The bailey was nearly empty but the noise of shouts and clanging metal from the upper bailey was deafening.

They looked at each other and walked straight on to the upper level. They crossed the grounds, passing the elemental fledgling houses and the House of the Dragon before they climbed the stairs leading them to the back of the grandstands of the arena. It looked like every single person on Fyra had gathered for the occasion, which they probably had. The entertainment for the day was a boy and girl, perhaps only about six or seven winters old.

Ward's mouth fell open and Sin bumped her fist on his arm.

"That boy," Ward said under his breath. "That's Roz's son. Ulric."

This was a deathmatch. Sin took a step forward and halted. It was too late to save him. One of the two combatants would die in the arena. If she intervened now, they would have already lost. She eyed the boy. Though young, his shoulders were already square and the muscles rolled under his lightly tanned skin. She remembered what Roz had said about his power, however, and passive powers were often weak when faced with someone who had a more practical skill set. The girl was surrounded by an emerald shade—her power was most likely bound to the earth. Sin gave the children about equal odds to win, though she wished none of them had to earn any marks this day. They were so close to liberating them all.

The sound of the gong reverberated up Sin's feet and the match began. Roz's boy was fighting with an ax and a shield. The girl had a shield, too, but carried a one-handed sword instead. The ax would do plenty of damage but the sword was easier to manage, and Sin favored it over the ax. The small combatants exchanged blows in a flurry of motions. The ground shook and thick roots burst forth at the girl's command. Ulric was quick to avoid them. His mind-reading placed him one step ahead of the girl at every turn. It reminded Sin of how she fought herself—she had a passive power like him. Perhaps he had an advantage after all.

The fight lasted a lot longer than Sin was used to. None of the two children was able to mortally wound the other. The crowd was cheering, yet at some point became impatient, and their cheers turned to insults and growling.

Someone tugged at Sin's cloak. The small girl from the Rite looked up at her. She held a hand over her mouth.

"They are friends," she whispered.

Sin shook her head. How had she not seen the horrors of the arena before now? There was no honor in killing, especially when your opponent was a friend. It reminded her of how she had killed Walis's daughter Sabine in the very spot where the combatants fought now. Sabine had been a friend as well, a close friend. Yet Sin had not hesitated the way these two did. Sin shifted her gaze over the assemblage to find the five masters.

Matteo had his eyes on her. His mouth was a thin line, his eyes motionless. There was nothing to tell how he felt about seeing her again. She could venture a guess, though. She forced a smile and received a tilt of his chin in return before he reverted his attention on the match.

The crowd roared and leaped to their feet before the gong bellowed to signal that the match had ended. A pit of blood spread slowly over the frosted sand to float over the sheets of ice. The light of the winter sun glinted on the edge of the ax, which was now embedded deeply in the girl's skull.

"Come," Ward said.

They turned away from the arena and found their way to the tower walk on the east battlements where Matteo had taken them that day they had met for the first time. It wasn't long before the Grand Master came to find them.

"Merry meet," Matteo said.

"Merry meet, Grand Master," Sin said, followed by Ward as he repeated the greeting.

"Sinyara!" Matteo's voice used to be calming. Now, however, it gave Sin shivers. She quenched the sudden desire to run away from him. "I'm so pleased you're back. It has been a while."

Sin bowed her head.

"And Ward. I'm glad to see that the two of you managed to find a way to work together." He chuckled.

"You received my reports?" Sin asked.

"Plenty of them. You've done a fine job." He spread his arms out. "You told me you took care of our problem. That was great news. And Everett tells me you saved him and Aisla as well."

"How are things on Fyra?" Sin asked.

"Much the same as always. You both look a little the worse for wear. Why don't you find yourself a bath and your beds, and we can talk more in the morning?"

That sounded just about perfect. Sin didn't want to explain herself, and the mere sight of Matteo made her want to stab him in the eye.

"Until tomorrow, then," she said.

Matteo nodded and walked away again. His cloak billowed around him as he disappeared into the nearest tower.

Sin drew the air into her lungs, supporting herself on her knees.

"That was rough," Ward said, mimicking her posture.

"You know what to do."

"Meet you at the stairs tomorrow." Ward sauntered along the battlements before he turned back. "Be safe. I couldn't bear to lose you."

Sin stared at him as he walked away, then darted up the walkway to find herself flying toward the stable.

"Shayfax?" she called. A comforting low whinny sounded from the booth at the end. Sin ran past the other stalls. She opened the latch and swung the door open. The two yellow unicorns turned their heads at her and Vilyur whinnied with delight. He had grown so much, his legs were strong, his coat shone and his silver mane reached all the way to his knees.

"Vilyur!" Sin sighed.

The young unicorn nickered. His horn had grown just above his ears. She smiled. Matteo had let it grow to give her the honor of sawing it off. She wasn't going to.

"Looking good," Sin said. "I hope you'll allow me to ride him?" she asked Shayfax. "I want to bring him with me to find my parents."

Shayfax nudged her with her muzzle. Sin looked into her eyes as she backed up, bowing her head. Vilyur stretched his front legs out and bent his neck. They were both giving her their approval.

She kept smiling as she stroked Vilyur's neck. "I missed you so much. I'm sorry I haven't been here."

She folded her hands around his cheekbones, placing her forehead on his, the edge of his horn resting on her head. She pulled back to look at the shimmering spear.

"I won't take your horn. I promise. You are a gorgeous, magical creature, and that horn is your birthright." Sin threw her arms around his neck and Shayfax placed her head over Sin's shoulders. They stayed like that for a while before Sin yawned and disentangled herself.

The unicorns looked at her like they understood everything, and perhaps they did. Sin found a curry comb and brushed Vilyur. The young unicorn raised his head and shook himself gently every now and again. He had not needed to be groomed but he seemed to enjoy it as much as she did. She placed the curry comb beside the trough before she arranged the balls of hay in the back of the stables. When her make-shift bed was done, she lay down and closed her eyes.

If Matteo wanted her dead, he knew where to find her. But he didn't want that—at least, not yet. He wanted her to open the gates and have the Children of Rhonja walk straight into the slaughterhouse. There wasn't a doubt in her mind that Matteo knew they were coming, and that Sin was helping them. It was all part of the plan. However, the plan had flaws. Once Sin had brought the Children of Rhonja through the gates, Matteo would find her and, when he did, only one of them would survive.

CHAPTER NINETEEN

S IN STARED DOWN AT E VERETT'S LIFELESS EYES WHILE sliding the dagger from his heart. She had not wanted to kill him but he would not have let her open the gates otherwise. He was the fifth Protector she had murdered before she arrived at the gatehouse.

She clasped her hands on the winch. The chains squeaked as the portcullis was raised as far as she was able before she ran to open the gates.

A rush of wind entered through the open gateway and lifted her cloak. The snow whirled on the ground before the sound of the gong rang and the ground began to shake. The Children of Rhonja flooded into the bailey as a large number of fledglings with a fair few Protectors among them came running down the stairs from the upper level. Their war cries filled the night. It was going to be a massacre, and although Sin was eager to join the fight on the ground, she had someplace else to be. She unsheathed her sword and dashed up the stairwell through the nearest tower, where she continued to sprint along the battlements to the east.

The sky was dark and the night was lit by a number of torches along the tower walk. Sin's breath turned to smoke as it met the coolness of the air. Two guards from the Children of Rhonja approached from the other end of the walkway.

They grinned at her.

Sin let her fingers glide over the pommel of her sword. She had known for a while that the two were not whom they appeared. But they had served their purpose and it had only been a matter of time before they revealed themselves. They could have stabbed Sin in the back weeks ago—or they could have tried—but their egos were too big to do so, and she had counted on them to tell on her.

"Hershel. Garreth. Did something go wrong with the illusion?" she called.

The guards laughed as their faces distorted and their bodies changed into familiar shapes.

Sin shook her head, feigning surprise. "I thought I left you in a dungeon."

The pink of Lacy's hair shone in the light of the torch beside her. "Stupid guards untied my hands to allow me to eat. And they took the scarf away from Mercy's mouth. She spat on them, of course, and from there the illusions have been easy. They look like us and we look like them. Well, they probably haven't looked like us for a while, and I thank the king we're back to looking like us again."

"You've been with us the whole time?"

"Honestly, Sin. Not much of a Seeker, are you?" Mercy snickered. "Your plan has failed. We sent a report with Nefero the second we departed that wretched island. The masters know everything, including your deceit and how you murdered Rip."

Sin clenched her jaw at the mention of Rip's name. "You never cared about him."

"More than you, it would seem."

"I loved him." The words slipped out, though Sin wasn't sure if they were true or not. Had she loved him? Was that a lie? She had cared about him, but love? Sane people didn't kill someone they claimed to love. Only someone as damaged as she could do something that cruel.

"You don't know the meaning of the word." Mercy angled forward, her shoulders rising. "You're a sinner; a killer like us. This is where you belong. Sadly, it won't be for much longer."

Lacy tossed her hair back. "Because you'll be dead."

Dead? Sin had no intention of dying. Certainly not by the hands of those rock-headed girls. The guards they claimed to have killed were very much alive. The girls had traveled with the Children of Rhonja ever since leaving the island, and yet they failed to see the truth. It was futile but Sin had to at least give them a chance.

"You don't understand. You both have parents out there, families, probably sick with worry about you."

"Our family is right here." Mercy held one arm around Lace, who blew her a kiss.

"If our birth parents wanted to come to claim us, they could have. But they cast us aside like rubbish. No, thank you. We don't want or need weak pathetic parents who didn't want us in the first place." Lacy was careless when her fingers wrapped around the hilt of her sword, revealing her next move.

Sin pretended to relax her shoulders. "You've improved, Lace. I have to hand it to you. This illusion has to be your best work."

Lacy sighed. "Told you I'm good."

"Also." Mercy rolled her eyes at Lace. "You're not the only one who came up with this plan. You had plenty of help."

"Well, it was mostly my design."

Good. They were bickering. Any distraction would serve Sin well at this point. They should have gone for the attack straight away, though it was less than surprising for Lacy to want to gloat about her almost perfect illusion.

"You're not as good as you think, Lace, but I don't want to kill you," Sin called.

"Like you killed Rip?" Lacy called back.

She should not have mentioned his name. Again. Sin had given them a chance; they refused to take it. She lunged forward as Lacy drew her sword. The ringing of blade meeting blade reverberated through her arm. The illusions were annoying but Mercy was the more dangerous one of the two. Sin stepped around Lacy and gave her an elbow in the back, making her stumble. It gave Sin a moment to focus her attention on the Venomizer.

Mercy smirked. Two daggers in her hands. She bent her knees, circling toward Lacy.

"Not another step," Sin said, thrusting her blade forward. Mercy parried with one of the daggers and plunged the other one into Sin's shoulder.

A searing pain shot down Sin's arm. She gritted her teeth, wrenching her arm back, the dagger still embedded into it. She swung her sword back around and split open the front of Mercy's top, leaving a red gash across her chest. It wasn't deep enough to stop her.

Mercy cleared her throat. She gurgled and spit at Sin, landing the charge in Sin's eye.

"Yuck," Sin exclaimed, wiping her eye with the back of her hand.

Mercy shook her head and took a step backward. "Why didn't you drop?"

"You can thank him." Sin angled her head at the tower behind them.

"Hi." The sound of Eamon's voice made Mercy cringe. He stepped out of the north tower, waving at them.

"But?" Mercy turned her head back and forth while Lacy scrambled to her feet beside her.

"I can take it from here, Eamon."

The boy nodded and scurried off into the shadows again.

Sin wasn't about to give Mercy time to find her bearings. She kicked Lacy back down as she tried to find her feet, jumped on her back and used the Illusionist's body to plunge herself into the air. Her blade bored into Mercy's skull, cutting through her head to sever her face and torso in half as Sin descended in front of her. Blood sprayed Sin's face as she pulled the sword free before turning to Lacy.

The girl trembled on her knees while Sin gritted her teeth at the throbbing of her shoulder. She had to leave the dagger in a while yet.

"Please stop. I'll do anything you want."

"I just killed your girlfriend. You'll come for me if I show you mercy now... no pun intended."

"I won't. I promise. Just let me live."

"You're too dangerous to continue to take breath."

Sin tiptoed, her right foot fell out in front of her, and she swung her blade again. It whistled as it cut the air before she severed Lacy's head from her body. Her body slumped and her head thumped to the ground beside her.

Sin stood for a moment, taking heavy breaths. She looked up and met Matteo's gaze as he exited the southern tower. He twirled two curved blades in his hands. From one problem to the next, Sin thought, and wiped her blade in the snow between the merlons.

"Give it up," she yelled.

"Fyra has stood strong for near on a hundred years, dear Sinyara. I'm not about to place it into the hands of a confused little bird like you." The tone of his voice was almost unrecognizable. There was a cold edge to it that Sin could not recall, though it had likely been there all along. She had simply been too blind to see it.

"You brought this on yourself then," she screamed. Heavy gusts of wind willed her to inch forward. "The Children of Rhonja are already inside. Let it go."

"My forces are stronger than yours."

"But they're not. Your strongest died shortly after Ward and I returned. We did not walk through the gates alone. The House Protectors died last night."

Matteo halted, raising his chin to the rain. "The House Protectors walked Fyra this very day."

"It turns out that there are a few Illusionists not in Fyra."

Matteo slid his foot across the snow. "It doesn't matter. I know you haven't killed any fledglings. You wouldn't. This is your home, Sinyara."

"This is a lie!"

The clash of blades from below whined in the night. Sin glanced down at the bailey. There were fights on both levels. The youngest children were already outside the gates, being led away from the fight to a clearing nearby. Hundreds of the Children of Rhonja charged the houses on the upper bailey, yet hundreds of fledglings had armed themselves heavily, eager to prove themselves. They wouldn't accept defeat without a fight, though they were lacking leaders. Taking out the House Protectors had been paramount. It left the fledglings to fight without direction, causing chaos.

"You tricked the trickster," Matteo wheezed. "You will die for this."

"If I have to."

He made the first move. He crossed his arms and folded them back out, the tips of his blades an inch from her neck as she jumped backward. She tripped over Mercy's body, landing in the pool of blood between her severed torso.

He came at her again. She rolled to the side just as his blade whooshed down, slush and blood splashing. The dagger in Sin's arm shifted and pressed deeper. She shook her head to overcome the sudden dizziness. She could pass out later.

Instead, she lunged out and spun on one foot, her head low. She drove her sword across the back of Matteo's knees. He wobbled on his feet but didn't fall. Instead, he turned to her and she spun back around, this time delivering a wide wound from hip to shoulder. He repented. She parried one blow but the tip of his other sword fell over her shin. It burned like her leg was on fire.

She gave a war cry, fighting through the pain, then clinked the pommel of her sword into his forehead. He fell to his back and dropped both blades. Flailing his arms, he searched for them, but Sin kicked them away. Standing over him, she pointed her blade to his heart.

"Enough," she said. "Tell me this is enough."

"Do it." He lifted his chest to press against the sword edge.

"I don't want to kill you. I'm giving you the chance for redemption."

"Redemption. Child, you have no idea. You'd best

end me now or believe me, this will be your last day on Aradrian soil."

She did believe him. It felt like Rip all over again. Matteo had committed atrocities beyond her imagination, however. Of that she was sure. But he had been her only constant for nearly thirteen years. He had tended to her wounds, played cards with her, taught her songs and shown her how to forge a blade. He had been her father in all but name. He had also taught her how to kill, how pain was wrong, and how she was an abomination and a threat to Aradria. The last part might be true but only because he made her so.

"I hope you die in pain," she said. She moved her sword from his heart and let the tip cut across his throat, torrents of red spewing out. Matteo coughed, choking on his own blood.

"Weak," Sin muttered. She shook her head and ambled over to the merlons. Leaning forward, she searched the ongoing fight on the ground. Where was he? An array of colors flooded the darkness. It would be difficult to single out their opponents and not disable Magicals from Rhonja at the same time. They had done what they could, however, and most of their own Magicals fought further back. There were large numbers of Unspelled huddled in groups closer to the stairwell separating the baileys. She shifted her gaze.

Ward stood on the top steps while Eamon stood on the steps of The House of the Dragon across the courtyard opposite. A surge of energy folded out over the combatants. The magical lights extinguished one by one until there had to be a few hundred combatants who had now lost their magic, if only for a while.

The boys did good. The Children of Rhonja pushed the fledglings further back, and the few remaining Protectors were falling to the ground. They had wanted the fight to be non-lethal, if possible. Sin couldn't imagine how it had to feel for the parents down there to have to fight their own children.

The surge of energy pulled back as a number of colors reappeared. Sin shook her head at Ward then looked to Eamon. The boy was sprawled on the steps. He had pushed himself to his limits.

Roz came running up the steps to Eamon, and she wasn't alone; Walis ran right beside her. Stupid old man. What was he thinking? Roz dragged Eamon into the House of the Dragon by his arms. As it were, they would all be safer inside. A young fledgling lunged at Walis before he had a chance to follow his son and Roz through the doors, however. They exchanged a flurry of blows. Walis was surprisingly intuitive for a blind man, but he eventually stumbled backwards. Sin sucked air into her lungs. Stupid, stupid old man. She wanted to scream at him but to what use? It was difficult to make out exactly what was going on when the fledgling raised his arm, stabbing a dagger downward. His body sunk as the edge of a blade penetrated his back.

Sin exhaled, shaking her head as Roz reappeared. She kicked the fledgling aside, then pulled Walis with her behind the doors.

Sin couldn't blame Walis for wanting to protect his

son but his job was to heal—outside the walls—not expose himself here. They needed him. And come to think of it, so did she.

Sin turned on her heels to sprint down the stairwell in the closest tower and face the battle still going on in the courtyard. She stepped over a number of bodies. There were casualties from both sides littered on the ground. But The Grand Master was dead and all they needed was the heads of the rest of the masters. That had been a job for Arcus and his team. She hoped they would arrive with the heads soon.

Sin swung her blade repeatedly, handing out flesh wounds but no lethal blows. She had to get to Ward. He was too exposed out there on his own.

She pushed past a group from her own team as a Magical fledgling rushed out from the crowd to hurl himself at Ward. He angled toward his attacker and held one arm out. The blood-red magic around the child snaked its way from the fledgling and across the ground before it crawled up Ward's legs and disappeared into him. His body became encased by a multitude of vibrant colors. The magic danced on his skin.

The fledgling crouched, then plunged into the air. Ward spun around faster than Sin could blink. His fist pounded into the child, sending him flying back down. The fledgling got up and charged Ward again. Ward clapped his hands together and the child's hands went to his throat like he was suffocating. The fledgling fell to his knees, gasping for air he could not reach. Ward gave a wave of his hand and the fledgling's neck snapped.

What was he doing? He had not needed to kill the boy.

Sin met Ward's gaze but it was as if he didn't even see her. His eyes were dark, almost black. She drove her pommel into the head of an attacker, then another, as she stumbled forward. She parried another attack, ducked and swung her blade. She was surrounded by fledglings. She kept landing blows until she could once again focus her attention on Ward. Another two fledglings charged him. He picked up a couple of pebbles and flung them in the air. The pebbles went straight up, then turned and shot through the skulls of his attackers. The power of a Marksman; Rip's power. Ward possessed all their powers now.

Sin's throat clogged and her stomach revolted. This wasn't happening. Ward was good. He was everything she wasn't. Perhaps this was an illusion, too? Was someone trying to trick her? It couldn't be, however. Roz had disappeared with Eamon, and Sin had killed the only other Illusionist she had known.

The shades around Ward multiplied while the ones on the battlefield diminished until Sin could no longer see any colors at all. This had not been the plan. He wasn't just killing fledglings and Protectors at this point, he was hurting the Children of Rhonja as well.

"Stop it!" she bellowed. "Ward! Stop it now!"

Ward stared blankly ahead. Anyone who dared to come close was put down in all sorts of magical ways. He was a Bird one moment, a Boulder the next, and he was using the powers he'd gained for only one purpose.

He had to stop. Or be stopped. A tear trickled away from the brim of Sin's eye. Magic had corrupted her best friend. Even the strongest, most benevolent among them was not immune. She cried out in pain. Not physical pain, but the kind of pain that felt like someone had wrenched her heart from her chest. Her shoulders rose and her back arched. She trampled over the bodies ahead until she was only a few steps away from the stairwell where Ward was.

"Please stop!" she screamed.

Ward tilted his head, his arms falling.

Aislin, Everett's teammate, was swinging a dagger in her hand. She was about to throw it when Ward's arms lifted again, his attention shifting to her. He rolled his wrists and Aislin froze mid step. There was no time to wait for a better moment. Sin couldn't hesitate. She bounded forward, embraced Ward, and drove her sword into his back. Aislin thumped to the ground as Ward turned, the black in his eyes vanishing as he stared at Sin.

"Sinyara." He gasped.

"Shush." Sin sniffled, taking him gently back in her arms. "Your parents will know how incredible you were." Tears streamed freely down Sin's face.

"Sinyara," he said again. "You had to."

"I know."

"I became a... an animal."

Sin shook. She wrapped her arms around him. His breathing slowed and then his heart stilled. She stood, wiping her tears. It wasn't over yet.

Arcus and his team came running through the courtyard.

Sin swallowed her sorrows and cleared her throat before she shouted at Arcus, "You have them?"

"All four heads. You've taken care of the last one?"

"Up there, on the east battlements," Sin said.

Arcus and his team fought their way through the throng of fighters until three of them reached the tower. They disappeared into the darkness, only to reappear at the top a short while later. One head after the other was mounted on a spike, along with their cloaks, which carried the coloraturas of their house. Matteo's head sat in the middle, his face distorted. Even in the night, the silver tint on their skin gleamed.

This was it. She took to her heels and dashed for the arena. Unlike the day before, the place was empty. The sounds of the battle seemed distant and subdued as Sin set her gaze on the gong.

She grabbed the gong hammer and inhaled sharply. The blood pumped wildly through her veins as she gathered all her strength and slammed the hammer on the gong.

The sound echoed over the mountaintop. She slammed it again, then once more, before heading back.

"Lay down arms," a voice boomed through a horn. Arcus was standing on the battlements. "Your masters are dead. Lay down your arms and we will not harm you."

The fighting had ceased. It was as though the world stood still. The shadows of Vulkan eagles in the distance sailed silently around the peak of the mountain, and the cold wind turned to a chilling whisper. The fledglings had to know they had lost?

Killing the masters was the only thing Sin had thought of that could stop the bloodshed but it was never certain that it would be enough. Concealing Arcus and his team with the help of Roz's illusion had given them the advantage they needed. Sin glanced at the faces of the fledglings, her gaze gliding over the few Protectors left among them. It was clear that they were not prepared for defeat. Why would they be? Fyra didn't teach them to lose, it taught them to win. None of them knew how to handle the situation and their House Protectors could not guide them anymore. They would need further persuasion.

Sin found her way to the House of the Dragon and peeked inside.

"Roz?"

"Here," replied Roz.

"Could you get me a horn. There should be one at the podium."

It didn't take long before Roz appeared with a horn. She placed it in Sin's hand and hurried back inside.

"Fledglings," Sin called through the horn. "Your masters are dead, your House Protectors are dead. You will die too if you do not lay down arms. But we do not wish your deaths. You have all been fooled. I was like you but I have seen the truth. Your opponents are your mothers, your fathers. They never wanted you to come here. Lay down arms and we will show you the truth. No one else will die tonight."

A breath of silence spread as Sin held her breath.

A single clank issued from somewhere on the steps between the baileys and a loud sob followed. The crowd shifted their heads this way and that before another sword fell—then another. The sound multiplied as one by one swords, daggers, shovels and whatever other weapons the fledglings had used, dropped to the ground. Some cried and a few still resisted. But it was over. Sin sank down, the stone wall at her back. She had survived, yet so many had not.

The temperature was rising as the rays of the morning sun made its appearance. Crystals of white fell from the sky. The snow would help wash away rivers of blood and leave the battlefield looking less horrific. It would not conceal what had happened entirely, and it would not wipe clean the damage they had caused or the lives that had been taken.

Eamon limped outside and Sin took the time to look at him now. His red hair was darkened and his face was smudged with blood, much like she assumed her own was. He had rips and tears all over his clothes and a deep gash down his left leg. Someone had given him a cut above his eye as well. Nothing too serious by the looks of it.

"Where's your father?"

Eamon sat next to her, breathing deeply. "A couple from Rhonja came to carry him to the infirmary out the back. He was in bad shape, Sin..." He shifted his gaze around before looking up at the east battlement. "There are so many dead. They're everywhere… You did all this?"

"I'm the true animal."

Eamon didn't argue. Instead, he cried. Sin bit her lip and fought the instinct to slap him over his head. Crying was a weakness. She slapped herself instead. Crying was not only for the weak. The strong could cry all the same. It didn't make them any less than the next person. It was a human emotion, and those were things to cherish. That was where the masters had been wrong. Training young Magicals to be cold and emotionless only pushed them further towards the edge of madness.

Sin wept, feeling more human than she ever had before.

They sat for a while, both weeping and comforting each other. They sat until the sky cleared and the snow stopped.

Eamon wiped the last tear from his cheek when Roz came to sit beside them. She clasped a hand under Sin's chin, turning her head this way and that.

"You've got some pretty deep wounds," she said. "I'm guessing the infirmary is full, though you need to get them cleaned and wrapped up. And that dagger in your arm has to come out as well." She put a hand on Eamon's shoulder. "We need to check on your father, too."

"Eamon has a few injuries himself," Sin said. "You did a great job with the illusions."

"It was tiring, I'll tell you that much. I can't cloak an

entire castle but a team of six was manageable enough."
She skipped down the steps. "I'm going to go help out
in the infirmary. You're both coming with me."

Sin stood and nearly dropped back down. Her head
spun and her eyes blurred. She had not allowed herself
to feel the excruciating pain in her body, and now it was
as though there was nothing left but pain.

Eamon wrapped his arms around her to steady her,
and they crossed the battlefield together.

CHAPTER TWENTY

THE INFIRMARY WAS PACKED. WELL OVER A COUPLE OF hundred people occupied the beds or lay strewn along the walls on mattresses and a variety of blankets. The room already carried the stench of death.

Eamon sped up and ran for one of the beds while Sin and Roz followed.

"Father," he sobbed. He looked back at them with bloodshot eyes.

Walis was on the bed. Two dark empty sockets had taken the place where his eyes had been. A deep gash went from one of his shoulders to the other, but a slight rising of his chest made Sin relax her shoulders. At least he was alive. He had not been supposed to fight, and though Sin wanted to be angry about that, all she felt was concern.

Roz gasped and leaned over Walis. "We need to clean and bind his wounds. Now." Her voice trembled.

"Will he make it?" Eamon asked.

"Your father is the strongest man I have ever known," Roz said.

Sin put her throbbing head in her hands while Roz bound Walis's wounds and Eamon sat by his side, holding onto his father's hand.

Arcus came by just as she had finished. "Roz," he said.

She looked up and her eyes set on the boy Arcus had brought with him. "Ulric!" She lifted the boy into her arms, swinging him around.

The boy, however, was rigid in her hold. She put him down and he tilted his head back at Arcus. "You say she's my mother?"

A knot formed in Sin's stomach. Such a cruel thing it was to make a child forget his mother.

Roz took Ulric's shoulders. "Look at me," she said. "I know you don't remember, but I do. We'll figure this out."

"Go on," Arcus urged.

Roz and Ulric stepped away, leaving Walis's bed.

Arcus sighed. "I'm glad she has Ulric now. I didn't have the heart to tell her that I couldn't find Hannah. I don't think she still lives." He crouched next to Eamon. "Do you need anything? Are you injured?"

"I only need my father."

"Nothing more we can do," Sin told Arcus. Her voice was hoarse and every word sent torturing jolts through her limbs.

Arcus was clearly hesitant. "Do you want us to stay?" he asked the boy.

"No. Go on. I'll be here," replied Eamon.

Sin and Arcus left Eamon and found a spot between a couple of occupied beds. Sin studied the man in front of her. Only weeks ago he had almost attacked her for who she was. Now he was tending to her wounds—and she, his.

He gathered a heap of bandages to wrap around the dagger, binding her shoulder tight.

"We need to take this out now."

"I know."

He cut a piece off his belt and placed it between Sin's teeth. They stared at each other for a moment before a searing sensation of agony rippled through her bones. Warmth spread as the blood flowed down her arm and she pressed her teeth together while the screams stuck in her throat. The world faded for a moment but she managed to stay conscious. She eventually spat the leather from her mouth, heaving for breath.

Arcus tossed the dagger aside and quickly put pressure on the wound. Sin swayed and the pain was replaced by a prickle on her skin, which soon turned to numbness.

"I'll bind it next. I think I can safely say you're the first I have treated for this kind of wound who did not pass out."

"Thank you," Sin stuttered.

However grateful she was for his help, it was an odd thing to sit there with Arcus when this moment should have been for Ward.

"You'll be all right now." Arcus smiled half-heartedly. "It's going to leave a pretty hefty scar but it seems you were lucky. And it has ruined your dragon mark. Just as well, I suppose."

It had what? Sin had a moment of regret and she swallowed back a sob. She shook herself. Why did she feel this way? The dragon was a mark of her days spent living a lie. She should be glad it was ruined. There was some part of her, however, who mourned what had been. The dragon would have been a reminder.

Arcus bound her shoulder as tightly as he could, clearly oblivious to her inner conflict. "There. All done."

"I appreciate it. All of it."

He nodded. "Now, I have a daughter of my own to find." His smiled broadened into one of genuine hope.

"Go get her."

Sin scrambled to her feet. Hundreds of wounded surrounded her. The Children of Rhonja had prevailed, but at what cost? The smell of herbs and iron invaded her nostrils and the air thinned. She had to get out. She moved as fast as she was able, forcing herself to keep going, despite the growing pains returning to her body.

She made her way to the stables and stumbled into the back stall where she crawled forward until she found her makeshift bed and climbed on top of it.

The unicorns neighed quietly but Sin had already closed her eyes. She could pass out now.

Gusts of wind rolled over the stables as she awoke. How long had she been out? Did it matter?

Vilyur stood over her, nudging her with his muzzle.

"Hey there, beautiful," Sin cooed.

The aches in her body made violent protests as she went over to the trough to splash water on her face. A horn file lay on the edge of the trough. She glared at it, then snatched it up. Turning it in her hand, her mind raced to make sense of everything that had happened. The image of Ward on the steps before she killed him kept repeating itself in her mind. She knew what she had to do.

"It's for your own good." Sin sniffled and brought up the file for Vilyur to see.

He whinnied and backed up.

"It doesn't hurt one bit. Look at your mother. Shayfax doesn't have a horn either, and this will make you stay sane. Please."

Vilyur bowed his head and motioned closer. When they were done here, Sin would take him to Yirin's stables at the foothills of Mount Fyra to train him.

Shimmering specks of light rained over her as she sawed away Vilyur's horn. She kept going until it was well beneath the tips of his ears, then pocketed the file and gave the unicorn a hug. She had lost so much to the curse of magic, and she wasn't about to lose him too.

"We leave soon," she whispered before she left the stable.

The air was misty and cool, soothing her skin and lessening the fiery pain in her body. The upper bailey was crowded with Magicals and Unspelled. Bodies were carried off and the level was nearly cleared of victims. Sin lingered, then decided they could manage without her for now.

She turned away and found herself on the trail behind the houses that led to the Dragon's Den. The last time she had walked this path was with Matteo. She remembered the feeling she'd had. The feeling of respect, companionship, and even love. And now he was dead. Lacy, Mercy, Rip and Ward were all dead, too. All of them killed by her hand. She cringed. It had been the right decision every time. Except, maybe, for Rip. He had been right all along. Perhaps not about killing Walis, but his intentions and instinct had been on point. One day she would return to the island where Rip was buried, and although she wanted that so much it hurt, it would have to wait.

Though Sin believed kidnapping children and training them to become assassins was wrong, she also believed that magic was treacherous. It didn't matter how pure a heart was to begin with, or how strong of will it was. In the end, magic would always consume its host.

The battlements ended to meet with the edge of the mountain by the Den. Sin angled away from the Den and moved onto the tower walk. She stared out over the merlons when Nefero sailed through a cloud to land on the rails beside her.

"Hey there," Sin said. She couldn't look at him the same way she had. He was as much a traitor as she was.

She had always thought she could trust him, that he was simple and loyal. All the while he had never been hers, nor had he been free; he had been Matteo's bird, trained to do what he wanted. The falcon had called her out from her hiding place, shown Matteo where to find her so her former Grand Master could take her from her parents and bring her to Fyra. She narrowed her eyes at the falcon.

Nefero squawked quietly. His beak lifted and fell. Sin retrieved a handful of seeds and the bird stuck its beak down while she stroked his feathers. Her fingers slid over Nefero's head and around his neck. Then she squeezed. Harder. Nefero squawked loudly and his wings fanned out, frantically trying to take off. She held the falcon down with a firm grip. The bird seeds rolled from her palm as she closed her hand around his eyes and beak.

"Shh," she said. Then she snapped Nefero's neck. She took a few quick breaths before she threw the bird out over the edge and watched him sail down the ridge of the mountain.

A tear swam over the brim of her eye and she sniffled. The masters were all dead. Mount Fyra was no longer the place where she grew up. Once everyone left the castle, the Children of Rhonja would level the houses, the arena; everything would crumble to the ground.

The Silverlings would still be serving the king, however. His mission to rid the world of Magical enemies would not change because of this one loss. He had other ways to achieve his intentions. Sin wasn't sure if his intentions were a cause for concern or if maybe the High King had the right idea all along. Perhaps he simply needed another means of executing his plans. She intended to find out.

First, though, she had to train Vilyur and find Ward's family. His real family. If nothing else, they deserved to know the kind of man their son had become before the darkness had consumed him.

She already knew his parents were alive. She had no idea if hers were, and the only way to find out was to travel to her birth land, Êvina. She would travel to the Land of Spirit, but not to find her parents. They didn't need to know what she had become. Her eyes were set on the vibrant castle of light she had read so much about, the castle where the king resided.

If what Sin had been told by Walis was true, the High King was a sorcerer, one who had succumbed to the darkness a long time ago, which meant he posed the biggest threat to the Unspelled of Aradria. Sin's mission in life had not changed. She was what she had always been and she would continue to serve her purpose until the claws of magic ran too deep, as they would with all Magicals.

Threats had to be eliminated.